Praise for Rachel Cord

Life's A Bitch. So Am I.

"An engaging hard-boiled adventure with a memorable protagonist." ~ *Kirkus Reviews*

"Nothing like this ever happens to Kinsey Millhone." ~ *Dianne K. Salerni, POD Book Reviews & More*

"(S)olid and complex . . . loaded with well defined and interesting characters." ~ *Rainbow Reviews*

Still A Bitch

"(M)y favorite mystery authors are James Lee Burke, Dick Francis and Tony Hillerman. Conary brews a plot to compete with these three." ~ *Lloyd Lofthouse, POD Book Reviews & More*

"R. E. Conary writes a really cool series about a female PI." ~ *Jochem Vandersteen, Sons Of Spade*

Rachel Cord Confidential Investigations Novels

Life's A Bitch. So Am I.

Still A Bitch

Bad Bitch Blues

Queen Of Tarts

Visit Rachel Cord at www.rachelcord.net

RACHEL CORD

Confidential Investigations

Bad Bitch Blues

R. E. Conary

Everyone Deserves An Equal Footing

Second Edition

Bad Bitch Blues

RACHEL CORD
Confidential Investigations
Book Three

Equal Footing Books
ISBN-13: 978-0692759417
ISBN-10: 0692759417
Copyright © 2016 R. E. Conary
Cover Illustration © Jo Ann Snover | Dreamstime.com
Title page illustration Apres Matisse

Previously published (2013) as
Rachel Cord PI and the Bad Bitch Blues

This edition includes an excerpt from
the upcoming Rachel Cord Confidential Investigations mystery
Queen Of Tarts
Copyright © 2016 R. E. Conary

She got the Bad Bitch Blues
Said, She got the Bad Bitch Blues
Oh, better take warnin'
Better take heed
Listen to me — I tellin' it true
Don't mess with no woman
Got those Bad Bitch Blues

One

Something angered Jean Watson. You could see it in her set jaw, tight lips, the concentration she gave her computer screen, the way she attacked the keyboard.

I was pretty certain that something was me. Not that irritating her was my sole intent, but I purposely arrived earlier than expected.

Perhaps it was my pale jade silk dress: too short—too sexual—for an afternoon business meeting. For the fourth time, I crossed my legs and tugged at the hem that barely reached mid-thigh. Perhaps it was my over-sized bosom straining the material. I sighed and breathed deeply— enhancing the effect—as I laid aside the magazine I'd been pretending to read. I took a soft leather case from my Vera Wang bag, laid the open bag on the floor beside the chair and stood up. From the case I took a gold lighter and a Sobranie Black Russian cigarette and turned to admire a painting on the wall.

"No smoking allowed in this building."

Watson's voice was grating and barely civil as she enunciated each word. Yes, she was definitely irritated. I looked at her over my shoulder. Jean Watson: executive assistant to Paul Danzigar of Romer Bartlett Danzigar & Tate; 27, 5 feet 5 inches; Single. Recently presumed pregnant according to the test kit found in the bathroom trash of her apartment. A dark-haired, dark-eyed beauty whose features were marred at the moment by a hateful glare. Too bad. Another time, another place . . .

"Ah am s-o-o-o sorry. Silly me. Ah forgot." I poured as much slow molasses as possible into the Biloxi accent I was affecting.

I turned back to the painting tugging again at the hem of my dress. Feeling daggers in my back, I sashayed to the window and glanced down at City Hall and City Park as I replaced the lighter and cigarette in the leather case. The sky was clear, the trees fully leafed out with spring color; rows of daffodils circled the central fountain. Leaning against the window frame, I watched Jean Watson ignore me. Her intercom buzzed.

"Mr. Danzigar will see you now, Miss Grey."

"Thank you so much."

Before Jean Watson could rise, the inner office door opened. Paul Danzigar stood in the doorway. Paul Danzigar: 48, 6 feet 1 inch; Married. Athletically trim: racquetball twice weekly, golf on Sunday. Styled dark hair going gray at the temples. Paul Newman eyes. Clean-shaven. Strong jaw. Flashy smile. University of Missouri and Harvard Law School. Three children. Only the youngest, Tara, 16, still lived at home.

"Sorry to keep you waiting, Miss Grey. Please come in."

He stayed in the doorway and my out-sized bosom nearly brushed his coat. I reached out and smoothed his lapel. It can be an innocent gesture with no meaning or—depending upon time, place and audience—one that conveys a certain intimacy generally reserved for spouse or lover.

"Shaaa-let, please."

"Right, Charlotte. Miss Watson, hold any calls."

I gave Jean Watson a sly smile and half-wink. Her face turned beet-red; hope I hadn't caused her apoplexy. After the door closed I heard in the receiver tucked in my ear her mutter, "Fucking bitch," and the pounding sounds of her fingers again attacking that poor keyboard.

Danzigar and I went thoroughly through the documents he had prepared. I slowly stretched the 15 minutes this appointment called for into 45. He made notes of several changes I requested.

"Ah hope that those changes won't be a bothah."

"Not at all; shouldn't take long."

"Ah have other appointments Ah must keep and won't be available this afternoon. My flight tomorrow leaves quite early. Could *someone* bring the papers to my hotel suite tonight for me to sign?"

"No problem at all. I'll bring them myself. Perhaps we could have dinner after?"

"That would be so wonderful. Say 7:00?"

"Fine. I look forward to it."

I moved close and brushed a bit of non-existent lint from his shoulder.

"Me too. Thank you, Paul, so much for all of your hard work."

Danzigar handed Watson the folder as we left his office.

"There are changes Miss Grey needs right away. They're marked."

I let Watson see me adjust the top of my dress and pull at my hem as I picked up my coat from the chair and sashayed to the outer office door. I patted my hair into place and turned.

"Ah look forward to dinner, Paul. And thank you, again."

The door was barely closed before I heard Watson explode in my ear receiver. I moved down the hallway and stopped to look at another painting and listen.

"What did that bitch mean about dinner, *Paul*?"

"Quiet down, Jean. She could have heard you."

"I don't give a damn."

"It's business. She leaves tomorrow and needs to sign these papers tonight. We're having dinner at her hotel is all."

"Dinner, right! I just bet that's all. If you think I'm letting you cheat on me with that balloon-titted bimbo—"

"Cheat? Jean, please. This is business. You can't possibly think that I'm interested—"

"The hell I can't. Wipe the drool off your chin. It's bad enough I've waited two years for you to divorce your wife, but if you think I'm going to bend over and—and another thing. I've got to see you tonight. There's something important *we* need to discuss."

"I'm sure there is, darling, but not tonight."

"Paul, please—"

"Wait, Jean. We have to wait. Just a little longer, I promise. The timing's not right for a divorce. We can't afford it yet. There are still too many assets that Valerie can find. I know it's hard for you. You think it hasn't been hard for me?"

I knocked and opened the door.

"Ah am so sorry. Ah forgot my purse. Silly me."

I picked up my bag from beside the chair and immediately left for the elevator. The elevator doors closed as I reached in my bag to shut off the transmitter and recorder. I looked in the mirror on the elevator wall: Marilyn Monroe-styled platinum blonde wig, smoky eye shadow and kohl-lined eyes, a dress that barely contained my—okay, my breasts are huge. Double-H huge, but balloon-titted? Hey, lady! This is all me: all natural, nothing artificial. I hate my breasts, they're a strain and a pain, but I hate even more when they're insulted. Balloon-titted indeed. Well, that was one problem that was soon going away. In a few weeks it was off to Florida and the reduction mammoplasty I'd craved for years.

Bimbo? She called *me* a bimbo? That's like—okay, Charlotte Grey's a coquette. A Deep South, sweet syrup-

4

tongued flirt from Biloxi whose purpose is to mislead, misdirect and see which way the winds blow. But she's no bimbo—I don't do entrapment. As Paul Danzigar would discover when his "just a little longer" came sooner than expected, and he arrived at my suite tonight to find, not Charlotte Grey, but his wife, Valerie, her lawyers and the evidence I'd collected over several weeks.

The elevator doors opened three floors down at the law offices of Marston Marston & Associates. I walked over to the receptionist.

"Rachel Cord to see John Cartwright. I'm expected."

Two

The next morning I walked to the second floor of the west wing of the Mann Avenue Plaza feeling much more comfortable in my double-breasted powder blue suit with dark blue shirt, tie, display hankie, black flats and topped with a neutral-colored, snap-brimmed Panama with a dark blue band. My somewhat butch look was softened by longer than shoulder-length hair returned to its natural straw blonde, a touch of lipstick, blush and subtle eye shadow.

The Mann Avenue Plaza is an old U-shaped high school building fitted around a large courtyard that was redeveloped into offices in 1990. I moved in in February '98 when I started Confidential Investigations, my one-woman operation. At the top of the stairs, Mary Farr and Doris Garrity were at the round reception center in the hall. Mary and Doris provide secretarial services to many of the small businesses on the second floor, including mine.

"Good morning, Rachel. You're looking snazzy. This your Easter outfit? Any special plans?"

"Morning, Doris. No, just my Marlowe spring look from *The Big Sleep* and no special plans. Wendy and I may just lie in the sun and read tomorrow; have Easter dinner with Wendy's mom on Sunday. You?"

"Bud's taking the kids fishing tomorrow so I'll have a day for me. Sunday we'll have a big Easter fish fry in the afternoon

7

after the neighborhood egg hunt."

Mary handed me folders and the morning mail. "It's sunrise services and Easter brunch for us. There are three final checks in there. You have four accounts still pending, and we sent the Rizelli brothers a third notice."

"I think their restaurant closed. The up-front grand may be all I ever get from them."

I opened the top folder, endorsed the three checks and deposit slip: $3,700 to the good. Ka-ching! The next folder contained two bills from F&G Secretarial Services and Mann Avenue Plaza, Inc. There were also two checks with my letterhead to pay those bills. Easy come, easy go. I signed the checks and gave the folders back to Mary. A third folder held my copies for filing.

"Is it true, Rachel, that you're closing down at the end of the month?"

"Just a few weeks for personal business. Can't afford to stay closed too long."

"Will you be around for your birthday?"

I felt the broad smile on my face. "Nope. I'll be in Florida for that."

Doris sighed. "Florida in May. Sounds like fun."

"Certainly hope so."

"You have one appointment scheduled at 11:00. Anything else?"

"No. I'm trying not to take on too much right now. Don't want anything hanging at the end of the month. I've a final report to write but should be done before the new clients arrive. Catch you later."

Like thousands of high school students before me, I walked the hall to Room 222. Many of these old classrooms were huge with two entrances, and to make affordable office space the developers split several into two offices each with its own entrance. Mine is like that: half a classroom yet still large

8

and light and airy with high ceilings and tall windows. I've kept the schoolroom look with a huge blackboard, a 1930s oak teacher's desk and two rows of three student tables where I spread the current case files and notes I'm working.

Only table 3 had anything on it: the Danzigar file. Usually two or three tables have something on them, and only twice in my nine years of business have I used all six tables at one time. By the windows at the front are two loveseats set in an L where I interview clients. At the back where the developers split the old classroom in half is a counter with microwave and coffee maker, cabinets above and drawers below, and a large storage closet. The closet holds filing cabinets, a few changes of clothes and a small safe.

I filed what Mary gave me and flipped through the mail tossing most in the trash and opening only a letter from the State Association of Private Investigators.

SAPI wanted all members to contact our state representatives and encourage them to pass the pending bill for statewide licensing of private investigators. It'd been a controversial issue for several years and this was the closest it'd been to passage. A lot of dinosaurs in the business considered it unnecessary government intrusion and thought licensing fees and regulation would be an unfair burden. Bullshit.

It was a simple matter of credibility. Anyone with a local doing-business-as license could claim to be a private investigator. There were no standards and even a concealed weapon carry license wasn't that hard to get. Flashing a mail-order tin badge and a photo-shopped ID doesn't get much respect in most professional circles. Most states require PIs to be licensed and have reciprocal agreements, so licensure could be a boon when crossing borders. It certainly would be for me as I often have reason to cross the river to our neighboring state. There were only six states left that didn't license PIs; hopefully, by year's end that would be down to five.

9

I pulled my laptop out of the desk, sent emails to my senator and rep, another to the mayor encouraging her support and copies to SAPI. That done, I started coffee, sat at table 3 with my notes, index cards and journal on the Danzigar file, and drafted a final report and billing statement. This didn't take long as I'd already given a final verbal report to John Cartwright at Marston & Marston.

I WiFied the report and statement to Doris and Mary for them to spell and grammar check and send out, filed my journal and notes, cleaned the blackboard and then settled onto a loveseat to catch up on the most recent *PI Magazine*. Articles on the CSI effect on criminal investigations, winning cases with hidden data, and teen investigations looked interesting. I read about a page before being distracted by two huge puffy clouds in the otherwise clear sky.

"**Y**ou're nearly 36," *Dr. Adam Brewster said, looking at my chart. "Why haven't you done this sooner?"*

"Insurance wouldn't cover the procedure, and I've only recently had the money and time."

"Should have done this years ago. Why not when you were in the Army?"

"Didn't think they'd pay for it, either. Thought it was considered cosmetic surgery."

"Enhancements are usually cosmetic. This they'd have approved. I mostly did reconstructive work on battlefield casualties when I served, but I also did several reduction mammoplasties."

"Now you tell me. Would have re-upped for that."

"Would have saved you years of discomfort, that's for sure. The good news is you're still a good candidate. Skin has good resiliency, only slight sagging — surprising considering your age and size. Do you tend to heal quickly?"

"Yes."

"That'll help reduce scarring. There will be visible scars as we

will need to reposition your nipples. You realize that, don't you?"

"Oh, yeah. I've looked at lots of pictures of before and after surgeries and read all the literature I could find. I know the risks, but these have got to go."

"What's your husband think?"

"My partner says, whatever makes me happy, makes her happy."

"Okay. You're not from Florida. There are many good plastic surgeons in your state. Why choose me?"

"Did a lot of research on the Internet. You have a good reputation, and I liked the after photos and testimonials of your clients. I also spoke with several of them."

"All right. Well, then, what size would you like to be?"

"Any chance of a B cup?"

"Hmmm. Could do it, if you insist. But with all the measurements we've taken and everything, I think aesthetically the smallest we should go would be C."

"I can live with that. When can we do it?"

"Let's check the schedule. How's May 4th sound?"

"Hmmm? That's the day before my birthday. Which makes that a Friday."

"Is that a problem?"

"Growing up my father said, 'never buy anything made on Fridays or Mondays. The mind isn't on the job; it's either waiting to start the weekend or recovering from the weekend.' I think he'd include surgeries in that opinion."

Brewster smiled. "I've never had that problem, but he has a good point. Tuesday the 8th is open. 8:00 a.m.?"

"Perfect. Lets – "

Three

The phone interrupted my thoughts. "Yes?"

"Mr. and Mrs. Perez-Carrera are here."

"Thanks. Send them down."

I stepped into the hall to await my visitors and was somewhat surprised to see two tall, blonde, blue-eyed Caucasians approaching. Had I passed them on the street I would have thought of Sweden, not Peru. The man's dark suit was clearly Armani, and the woman's jacket and skirt screamed Oscar de la Renta. I'd no doubt that her Gucci bag and shoes were real.

"Good morning, I'm Rachel Cord. Please come in."

"*Gracias.*"

"Thank you. I am Isabella Perez y de la Flores de Carrera and my husband, Raul Carrera y de la Castilla."

"Pleased to meet you. We can sit by the windows. Would you like some coffee?"

"No, thank you."

"*No, gracias.*"

I opened a new journal to take notes. "Yesterday when we spoke on the phone, you said that your daughter Maria had run away, is that correct?"

"We are Maria Salvador's legal guardians here in the States, but she is like a daughter to us. Her parents, Dominga and Hector, work at our family estate in Lima. Maria and our daughter, Elena, have been life-long companions. When it was decided we would come to the United States for a period, we offered to bring Maria also."

"I see. What exactly do you do?"

"Our families own an export/import business. It is our time to run the U.S. side of the business. I manage our retail store here. We also have family-run branches in Oregon and New Jersey. Raul is in charge of the flow of all goods between our countries. He is also a consultant and advisor to the Peruvian consul here."

"How long have you been in the States?"

"Nearly four years. This summer is our last. We return to Lima before fall and cousins will take our place."

"Okay. Did you bring a picture of Maria?"

"Yes, as well as the list of homes and places she is allowed to visit on her own, as you requested."

"Thank you."

Maria had long black hair and dark eyes, well-defined features that clearly showed her Incan as well as Spanish heritage and a magnetic smile. She wore a white and red party dress.

"She's quite pretty."

"That was taken when she turned 13."

"When was that?"

"Last year. August 8."

"When did you discover that Maria was gone?"

"Wednesday morning when she did not appear for breakfast."

"Any idea as to why she would run away? Trouble at school, for example? At home? Drugs or alcohol? Would you say she was a happy child?"

Carrera said something in Spanish too rapidly for me to follow, and his wife answered him back as quickly.

"Please excuse my husband; his understanding of English is far greater than his comfortableness to speak it."

"Certainly. I know my fourth grade Spanish holds up to only the simplest conversations. Please understand that though some questions may seem intrusive and personal, it's important to consider why Maria ran away. It's my experience that most runaways do so for similar reasons. Whether actual or only perceptual, the reasons are real and unique and seem overwhelming to the individual."

"I understand. No, I can't think of why she might run away. Definitely not drugs or alcohol, and I would have said that she was happy, yes. I know of no major troubles. However, late last year her schoolwork deteriorated, and her English became not so good. With the advice of the good sisters at Sacred Heart, we began home schooling her this year with the aid of tutors. She seemed to enjoy that, and I thought she was responding well."

"Are any of Maria's tutors men?"

"No. All three are women and approved by Sacred Heart. They are on the list I gave you."

"How would you describe Maria?"

"Quiet. Quite shy, really. Somewhat of a loner. But always willing to pitch in with chores or whatever's needed."

"Does she have a boyfriend?"

"No. She is much too young for that."

"Does she know you're returning to Peru this year?"

"Of course."

"How did she feel about that?"

"I would have thought excited. She misses her parents and brothers and sisters."

"Does she have computer access? A MySpace account, for instance?"

"Both girls have MySpace accounts, but we monitor those because of the talk we hear about exposure to pornography and pedophiles. I checked this morning but saw no new entries. The girls want to join Facebook, which is supposedly safer, but I'm not sure which is better."

"How about cell phones?"

"No. They have asked, but we have seen no need. They are too young, I think."

"When did you last see Maria?"

"Tuesday evening. She said that she was not feeling well and went to bed earlier than was usual."

"What time was that?"

"Before 8 o'clock, but I am not sure exactly."

"Did you check on her later?"

"No. This was a mistake, yes?"

"That's hard to say. You reported all this to the police?"

Carrera started again, but Isabella quickly raised her hand.

"Yes. Wednesday afternoon after we had called to everyone we could think of as to where she might be."

"Who did you speak with?"

"An Officer Brody in Missing Persons. She asked many questions. A patrol came later and gathered more information and a picture of Maria also. I do not recall their names."

"I've spoken with Officer Brody on other occasions. Is it possible Maria didn't leave voluntarily? That she was abducted?"

"I shouldn't think so, no. Who would do such a thing? Why? We are not so rich, I think, for ransoms. I cannot see how such a thing could be accomplished. We have a working security system; it was on when I came down to make coffee that morning at 6:00, and I turned it off then. Agueda Lopez, our housekeeper and cook, arrived normally at 6:30. She and I had our usual morning coffee together. At 7:00, she began preparing breakfast while I knocked on the girls' doors and went to awake Raul and dress."

"Who actually discovered Maria gone?"

"Elena. When Maria didn't come down, I sent Elena to get her. This was about 7:45. She came back saying she couldn't find her. We searched the house and yard. Her bicycle was still locked in its spot in the garage. Raul then went around the neighborhood in the car to see if she possibly went for an early walk and Agueda and I had not noticed her leaving. When he returned, we started calling around. I kept Elena home from school to help."

"Do you recall if Maria's bed looked slept in, or was made-up, or was stuffed with something to look like she was there sleeping?"

"The bed was made. Maria is very good at making her bed promptly and keeping her room neat. Elena, not so neat."

"When did you turn the security system on the night before?"

"I usually set it at 11:30 after the news program when I go to bed. Yes, that is when I did it. Raul stayed up for awhile, there was a program on Univision he wanted to see, but I went to bed as usual."

"Do the girls know the security code and how to set it?"

"I would think not, but it is possible."

"When Maria went upstairs, what were the rest of you doing?"

"Watching television in the family room. Elena was also reading her History book for homework."

"So Maria could have sneaked out anytime, but most likely left Tuesday night before you set the system, or in the morning after it was turned off."

"This makes a difference?"

"Mainly for me. It's a starting point. I don't know why she left or what her plan was—if she had a plan, that is. Knowing when helps me determine her options as to how, which—hopefully—will lead me to where."

"It is complicated."

"It can be. Do the people on the list know I may be contacting them?"

"Yes, we spoke with them, and they will help in any way they can, but none have any idea where she is."

"I understand. One last question: do you know how much money Maria may have with her?"

"I'm sorry, no. We give them a small amount each week to spend as they like, and each has a bank account, but I keep the ATM cards for those. I would think not more than $20."

"Okay. Here is my standard contract. If you would read and sign it and pay my basic retainer, I'll start right away. May I come to your home this afternoon? I'd like to see Maria's room and speak with your daughter."

Carrera said something, but his wife's raised hand silenced him before he finished. She signed the contract and handed me a check she had already prepared for $1,000.

"Of course. 4:30 would be most convenient. Elena will be home before then."

"Okay, see you then. Meanwhile, I'll spread the word on Maria. Maybe we'll get lucky and someone I know has seen her."

After they left, I sat staring at Maria Salvador's photo. She'd been given a wonderful opportunity, so why run away? As I had said to them, statistically teens run away for similar reasons: trouble at home which could involve disagreements over rules; or physical, emotional or sexual abuse, or neglect; trouble at school such as failing or dropping out, bullying or peer pressure; drugs and alcohol; relationships falling apart or someone missing or dead. Stress is often a factor. Not that statistics are necessarily to be trusted either. Didn't Mark Twain say something about "lies, damned lies, and statistics"?

Niggling thoughts tugged for my attention, but none came into focus. For some reason I didn't feel I was getting the whole story; perhaps it was just paranoia of not understanding their rapid Spanish, or as my favorite TV character, House, says, "Everybody lies." Hopefully I'd have a clearer picture after my visit.

As soon as the Perez-Carreras left, I created a case file folder, 2007-0406-1: Perez-Carrera, and scanned Maria's picture into my laptop with a few notes. Then I sent urgent emails to PJs, whose home in Lincoln Heights has served as a refuge for runaways for many, many years; to The Lillith Society, a local group started by two former sex workers to help keep young girls from becoming victims of the sex trade; to Ariana Feldman, who with volunteer help went around to homeless campsites giving out blankets, food, toiletries and sundries; and to Interfaith Harvest, a local charity that ran several hot meal sites and food banks. All were good sources of spotting runaways and had often helped me. I then ran off copies of Maria's picture with her description and contact information on the back for my own use and called Missing Persons.

"Officer Wainwright. How may I help you?"

"I'm Rachel Cord. Is Officer Brody available?"

"One moment."

"Hi, Rachel. Haven't spoken to you in quite some time. You looking for someone new or updating a cold case?"

"New, Denise. Maria Salvador. You spoke with her guardians Wednesday."

"Right. I take it she hasn't returned home yet."

"Not yet. I was just hired to look for her. Was an Amber Alert put out?"

"No. She didn't fit the criteria: no apparent abduction and she's over 12. Patrols have her picture, but no sightings yet— which isn't surprising. She looks a lot like any other Hispanic teen and few her age carry ID. Still, she's in the system at least, which is better than most, I think. You any idea how many supposed runaways out there were actually kicked out of their homes?"

"Way too many, I know that."

"You got that right. Wish we had the manpower to really look for them instead of being basically a listing agency."

"I hear you. Just wanted you to know I'm looking too. Any suggestions on new teen hangout spots?"

"Mercado Verde on the Westside is hot and not just with Hispanics; that's a long haul from where Maria lives, but I'd look there. Anyway, good luck to you."

I added my conversation with Denise to the Maria Salvador journal that I left lying on table 3 as well as adding Mercado Verde to my list of places to visit in my take-along notepad. I then called the families of Maria's friends from the list I'd been given. They were concerned but knew little to help me find the girl.

I turned off the coffee, put things away and was looking over a city map when my office phone rang.

"Rachel Cord. How may I help you?"

"Hey, Big Mama. This is Brownie. I was hoping to find you in."

Jeremiah T. Browne owned Brownie's Country Danceland, a Country Western club on Cutter Avenue with a mostly gay following. His place is decorated with gear and images of the Buffalo Soldiers of the 9th and 10th Cavalry regiments and black cowboys like Nat Love, Isom Dart and rodeo legend Bill Pickett. Brownie loves telling stories of the old west and how black men helped tame it. He gets away with calling me "Big Mama" because he's not referring to my over-sized bosom but to my *big* attitude as he puts it. Exemplified by my agency motto: *Life's a Bitch. So am I.*

"Hey, Brownie. What do you need?"

"Well, a coupla months back I opened a jazz and blues club in my basement below the Danceland. It's starting to draw a crowd thanks to a new singer I've got, Sunny Tristan. The thing is someone's trying to harass her, and I'd like to hire

20

you to check it out. Could we meet to talk it over?"

"I'd love to help you, Brownie, but I just started a new case, and I'll be tied up the rest of the day."

"How 'bout you catch her act tonight as my guest, and we talk between sets? Nuthin' else, you'll hear some great blues. She goes on at 9:00."

"I can do that. All right if I bring Wendy? She likes the blues."

"Your lady friend? Of course. I'd love to see her again too."

I pulled out a fresh journal and laid it on table 1 in case Brownie and Tristan became clients and called Wendy at her bank. She was in a meeting, so I left a message on her voice mail that we'd be going out that night and asking what she'd like to do for dinner. On my way out, I stopped and spoke with Mary.

"The final Danzigar report and billing are ready to go out. I doubt I'll be back today. Here are some notes on Maria Salvador, who the Perez-Carreras have hired me to find. If anyone calls about her or really needs to reach me, please have them call my cell. I'll keep it on."

"You've been doing much better about that."

"What's that?"

"Keeping your cell on. I can remember how hard it used to be to reach you."

"I still don't like it, but there are times now when I actually believe it's a necessity. Anyway, I'm outta here. Happy Easter."

"You too."

Four

The first thing I wanted to do was get a feel for the area where Maria lived. I drove north on Central Boulevard and felt a yen for an early lunch as I passed Charlie's Chicago Hot Dog Stand at the corner of Cutter Avenue. Charlie's dogs are works of art: over-sized, all-beef hot dogs served on toasted, poppy seed buns with yellow mustard, neon green relish, onions, chopped cucumber, tomato wedges, Greek peppers and sprinkled with celery salt. My personal favorite is Charlie's Slaw & Chili hot dog covered with his own non-mayo, non-dairy, yet creamy slaw and homemade chili. Very messy but, "Oh!" so good. Maybe later.

I continued north toward Old Town, turned west onto Martin Luther Parkway (so-named for the eight Lutheran churches along its length and not to be confused with Dr. Martin Luther King Jr. Avenue to the south that separates South Ferry and Lincoln Heights), then north again onto 21st Street which took me under the viaducts of South Main Street, the railroad tracks and North Main Street. This can be confusing as the two Mains actually run east-west parallel the train tracks and therefore should be "Avenues" and not "Streets." One councilmember suggested renaming them North and South Main Street Avenues. Doubt that would clear up the confusion.

The Amtrak station is still in Old Town, while the current

downtown, including City Hall, City Park, the new County Courthouse and Records building and such, are farther west. Twenty-First Street continues north until it ends at North Ferry Avenue but I was only going as far as Radford.

A 24-hour gas and convenience store and Belle's Diner sat at the northeast corner of 21st Street and Radford Avenue. On Maria Salvador's approved list was the JoAnne Frances Hanson Branch Library on the southeast corner. Across 21st Street were another gas station, Mama Rosa's Pizzeria and a Bank of America branch. Nine blocks west was St. Mary Magdalene Catholic Church and Sacred Heart School for Girls where Elena attended and Maria had been enrolled. Six blocks east was Radford Park, another of Maria's favorite places, and four blocks north from there was the Perez-Carrera home. I parked at the library.

Before going in, I went to the bus stop on the corner to check the schedule. The first bus going north stopped here at 7:25 a.m. and the last at 9:25 p.m. I crossed the street to check the south schedule: first bus was 8:05 a.m.; last bus was 10:05 p.m. Whether Maria sneaked out early enough before the security alarm was set Tuesday night or first thing Wednesday morning, she could easily have caught a bus here. Otherwise, she'd have had to walk away or had another option. Bus drivers were added to my list of interviews. I wrote down the route number to check end destinations and went back to the library.

In the library entry among other free literature was a display of bus schedules. I picked the one I wanted. The route originated at the downtown terminal and ended at Westbrook Mall on North Ferry Avenue. There was also a schedule for the Loop bus that I knew stopped at the mall. I took that too.

The woman at the help counter was about my age with dark hair done in a French braid. She was working at a computer terminal. I showed her Maria's picture and my business card.

24

"I'm Rachel Cord, a private investigator. This is Maria Salvador, who I believe comes here often. She's been missing from her home since Wednesday morning. I've been hired by her guardians to locate her. Have you seen her recently?"

The woman pulled out a flyer from beneath the counter that had the police logo and phone number along with Maria's photo and physical statistics.

"I know Maria and we've been alerted to her disappearance. I haven't seen her since Monday."

"What books has she recently read or have checked out?"

The woman made a few strokes on her keyboard and studied the screen for a moment.

"I'm sorry. Maria is 13 and her library card is in her name. It's a privacy issue. Unless she has a signed waiver listing a third party who may see her account—and I don't see one indicated—I can't give out that information.

"Surely if it would help find her—"

"I'm sorry. I understand. I'd like to help if I could, but ever since that god awful Patriot Act went into effect, our instructions have been crystal clear regarding our readers' privacy. I'm afraid it would take a duly served warrant, at least, and more likely a court order—which, from experience, I guarantee would be appealed—before that information is released."

"Is there anything you can tell me?"

She thought about it for several moments. "Maria is a bright, friendly, outgoing girl and a voracious reader. She comes in at least once a week and often twice or more. When she finds something she's interested in, she tries to get a Spanish translation at the same time as the English edition, if possible."

"When you say friendly and outgoing, how do you mean?"

"Usually smiling and she can be quite talkative about

subjects she likes. She's bent my ear many times, but it's a joy to see someone as enthusiastic about books as I am."

"Do you speak Spanish?"

"Heavens, no, but Maria has taught me some phrases. Her English is excellent."

"Really? It's my understanding her English is poor and she's quite shy."

"Not the Maria I know."

"Does she come in alone or with others? Does she meet anyone here?"

"Most often alone; sometimes with an adult, sometimes with another girl—her guardians' daughter I believe she once said—or a small group of girls from Sacred Heart. As for meeting anyone, I think she belongs to our Harry Potter Book Club. They meet here the second Sunday of every month at 3:00 p.m."

"Is there a contact name and number I could have for the book club?"

"Certainly." She handed me a flyer.

"Are You A Wizard Or A Muggle? Either Way, You're Welcome At HOGWART'S READERS GUILD. Join Us Every Second Sunday (3:00 p.m.) For All Things Harry Potter At The JoAnne Frances Hanson Branch Library. For More Information, Contact Becca Nichols (Hufflepuff) At 555-4321."

"Thank you. When you saw Maria most recently, did you notice any change in her? Stressed? Worried? Overly jubilant? Any change at all?"

"Not that I recall. Actually, now that you mention it, when she's with others she's more reserved, practically diffident."

"Ever see her with a boy?"

"You mean like a boyfriend?" I nodded. "No. Never."

"Thank you." I turned to leave, then turned back. "You can't tell me what she reads, but can you say how many books she has out presently?"

She looked at her screen. "Eight."

I now had two distinctly different Marias but saw no reason for Isabella or the library lady to lie. Was there a third Maria waiting to be found? I added this conversation to my notepad before I forgot anything then pulled across and parked between the convenience store and Belle's Diner. I went into the store.

The clerk was in his early-20s. Like countless others, his eyes went to my bosom before rising to my face. The shift was quicker than most—perhaps he didn't care for double-breasted suits.

"Hi, I'm hoping you can help me."

"How's that?"

I laid Maria's picture on the counter. "This girl has gone missing. Have you seen her any time this week?"

He pointed to a flyer on the wall behind him. It was the same one as at the library.

"Mr. Carrera dropped that off yesterday and asked the same thing. As I told him, I last saw her Monday afternoon. She came in and bought a candy bar. An Almond Joy, I think. Anyway, something with almonds. With her, it's always almonds."

"What about Tuesday night? Were you working then?"

"No. I normally leave at 5:00. Mr. Bharani, the owner, worked that night. It's usually him or his wife at night."

"I see that there are security cameras outside as well as in here. Do they work?"

"I certainly hope so, but you'd have to ask Mr. Bharani if you want to see the tapes."

"How can I reach him?"

"Come back later. He's on tonight. Usually he comes in

between 3:30 and 4:00 to check inventory, receipts and stuff."

"Okay, thanks. I'll be back."

I went next door to Belle's Diner. The smell of freshly-fried French fries hooked me right away and the sight of an old-fashioned milkshake maker sealed the deal. Charlie's Slaw & Chili dog would wait another day. The place was set up like a diner from the '50s: booths with red Naugahyde upholstery along the front windows; long counter with stools; circular pie display on one end by the cash register; four of those chrome-plated mini song selectors along the counter; a Wurlitzer jukebox at the far end by the bathrooms. Actually, a whole lot like the diner I used to go to growing up in Iowa back in the '80s. The song playing was *The Great Pretender*. I sat at the counter and picked up a laminated menu. Unfortunately, the prices were strictly 2007.

On the wall was a small chalkboard announcing "Blue Plate Specials: Chicken-fried steak w/gravy & 2 sides & drink, or BELT (bacon, egg, lettuce, tomato) Sandwich w/fries & drink—$6.95." Both were tempting, but nostalgia won out and I ordered a fries & onion rings basket and a chocolate milkshake.

As my order was being made, I thumbed through the song selections and was surprised that I could still get three songs for a quarter. For the atmosphere, I picked out *Crazy* by Patsy Cline; for my mom, Patti Paige's *Tennessee Waltz*; and for me, Chuck Berry's *Johnny B. Goode*—though my memories had more to do with the movie *Back To The Future* than Berry's original.

The milkshake was just as I had hoped: made from real ice cream served in a tall milkshake glass—not Styrofoam—with some left over in the stainless steel container set on the counter, and so thick I couldn't suck it through a straw but had to start with a spoon. The basket of rings and fries could easily feed three or four.

"Kin I getchya anything else?"

I asked for a saucer with some mayonnaise.

"Mayo?"

"A friend of mine's father learned to eat fries that way when he was stationed in Germany back in the '60s. She picked up the habit from him. Tastes a lot better than it sounds."

The waitress brought the saucer of mayonnaise, and I dipped a hot fry in it.

"Try one."

She gave me a tilted I-don't-think-so look and waggled her hand back and forth before going off to serve another customer who had just walked in, leaving me with my fries and memories of my first love, Betty Jean Cooper. I added a pool of ketchup next to the mayo. Mayo was always Betty Jean's thing more than mine.

We were giddy 15-year-olds back then and pretty much oblivious and naïve but knew we'd have to pretend we were interested in boys. Not that we fooled many people. Betty Jean and I were the *Big Scandal* of our sophomore year. The scandal and rumors quieted when, as juniors, we started dating and going steady with star jocks from the football and basketball teams, Dennis Kiley and John Lott. People assumed we had outgrown a rebellious phase. Then the rumors were more along the line of who would *have* to get married before graduation. Very few ever suspected that our double dates ending at Lovers' Lane involved a flip-of-a-coin or game of Rock-Scissors-Paper to decide who got the roomy backseat of John's old Chevy: Betty Jean and me or Dennis and John.

I had eaten all of the onion rings, a third of the fries and poured the last of the shake into my glass when the waitress came by carrying the dirty dishes left by the other customer. Sure enough, the blue-plate specials came on real blue plates.

"You gonna finish those fries or would you like me to wrap them to go?"

"Wrap to go, please. Thanks, Dot."

She looked at me quizzically for a moment then glanced down at her nametag.

"That who I am today?"

It was my turn to be quizzical. She laughed.

"We keep a box of tags with common waitress names from the '50s and just grab one when we come in. Last week I was Mary six days straight. Regulars know I'm Lisa."

"I'm Rachel. I see you have one of those missing girl flyers posted. I've been hired to help find her. Could I ask you some questions?"

"Sure. Just let me get rid of this stuff."

She took my basket and the shake container and came back a few moments later with the leftover fries in a paper bag.

"The fries are wrapped in foil, so don't worry 'bout any grease staining the bag or your car seat. Now, what do you want to know?"

"Maria Salvador, the missing girl, did she ever come in here?"

"Oh, yeah. Not every day or every week, but I'd say fairly often. Course I can only speak for the days I work, but I'd call her a regular."

"Would you know if she were in Tuesday night or Wednesday morning?"

"Kim and Patty were here Tuesday night. Patty closed. I opened on Wednesday, so I know she wasn't here then. Patty comes on tonight at 6:00. Being Friday, we're open 'til 2:00 a.m."

"Not sure I can get back here tonight." I wrote my cell number on the back of one of my cards and gave it to Lisa. "Give this to Patty, please, and ask her to call me if she can. It's important to know if she saw Maria or not Tuesday night. Or I'll try to call later. What's the number here?"

"555-1765. I'll give this to Patty."

"Thanks. When Maria is here, what does she usually

order?"

"Chocolate malted or sometimes a hot fudge sundae sprinkled with toasted coconut and chopped almonds."

"Is she usually alone or with someone?"

"Usually alone and usually with books she just checked out from the library. A few times with another girl. One of those from Sacred Heart."

"What's the girl look like? Do you recall?"

"Blue-eyed blonde, school uniform. Like half the girls I see from there, I guess."

"Maria ever with a boy?"

"Don't think so."

I paid for my meal adding in a larger than average tip for the information.

"Thanks, you've been very helpful."

"Glad to do it. Come back anytime."

I updated my notepad and drove to Radford Park. Supposedly the park was one of Maria's favorite places she was allowed to go. Not that that was significant: Belle's Diner wasn't on the list and apparently Maria went there regularly. Where else did she frequent that wasn't approved? It was only 2:30; Bharani wouldn't be in for another hour at best and I wasn't due at the Perez-Carrera's until 4:30.

The park was extensive and irregularly shaped: low rolling hills, woods, some spring flowerbeds blooming. A map of the park designated three major picnic areas with a phone number to call for large group reservations; there was an area for a softball/Little League field, soccer field, basketball and tennis courts and restrooms; also a children's playground. I glanced in that direction and could see some children scrambling about and mothers or nannies sitting nearby.

There were two walking/jogging trails: one a half-mile in length, the other 1.5 miles. The longer trail also allowed biking. There was a pond, but no fishing or swimming allowed. Two areas on the map were marked for development as a mountain bike trail and a skateboard park. The list of rules stated that the park opened at 9:00 a.m. and closed one hour before sunset daily except for scheduled evening sporting events; overnight parking or camping was not allowed. A nice, typical suburban park to my eye, but I didn't see the immediate attraction for a 13-year-old girl. Unless one were meeting an unknown boyfriend. Something I still contemplated.

Back in my car I drove southeast to the Postern home, one of her friends' homes that Maria could go to and the farthest from her house. The neighborhood was well-established cul-de-sacs of mostly two-story homes with garages beneath one end. Unlike its neighbors, the Postern's front lawn hadn't been recently cut or weeded and several shrubs needed pruning. I had no idea if that were significant or not or if—like me—the Posterns just weren't yard fanatics. I'd done enough yard and outside chores growing up on a farm to last a lifetime. That's one reason I own a condo and not a house.

I swung around and headed back. Crossing Radford the neighborhood changed distinctly: houses were larger and varied more in design, property lots were larger, and values probably jumped $20,000 to $50,000 more at least. I found the Kennedy, Upchurch, Gatwick and Perez-Carrera homes. The Gatwick home on a double or triple-sized lot with its gilded lions and wrought iron gateway seemed over the top and drew attention to itself.

I drove the obvious routes between Maria's home and the others a couple of times. If I could narrow the when, I'd have a better idea of who may have seen her. I headed back to see if Mr. Bharani was at the convenience store. He was, but he hadn't seen Maria Tuesday night. One of his sons fell downstairs and broke an arm that night, so he had closed the store shortly after 8:00 and hadn't gotten back to reopen until after 11:00.

"We needed to take him to hospital. I did not have time for replacement here."

"When you're closed, do you shut down the security cameras too?"

"No. We rarely close but have been robbed opened or closed. So our cameras are always on?"

"Who handles your security?"

"We have our own system."

Bharani's system was an old one consisting of two VHS tape recorders. One recorded the two in-store cameras and the other recorded the four outside cameras. The recorder for the outside cameras took a single picture every five seconds as it rotated between the four camera views. Each picture "frame" was time/date stamped in the corner, but it was disconcerting watching the four views flash by on playback. It didn't help that the tapes had been reused countless times. The quality was poor and nighttime lighting minimal.

At 8:20 p.m. — 04/03/07, a young woman or girl in a dark coat and jeans walked up to the front entrance. She wasn't carrying anything. Finding the doors locked, she stared through the glass for a minute or two and then walked to the northbound bus stop by the library. At that distance she was barely more than a darker shadow in the dark. Moments later the bus pulled up and she got on. It could have been Maria, although I was somewhat surprised at how early she would have needed to sneak out.

The bus ended at Westbrook Mall and that possibly could have been her destination. Though the mall closed at 9:00 p.m. on weekdays, the Cineplex-14 was open later. I went through my contacts to see if I had any current listings for Westbrook security. I didn't. I called Denise Brody.

"I'm following a possible sighting of Maria Salvador. Do you know anyone at Westbrook Mall security? I'd like to see their security videos for Tuesday night. Not sure that they'll just show them to me."

"Try Reed Hadley. He's head of security. When are you going out there?"

"I'm meeting with Maria's guardians in about 20 minutes and want to hit the mall right after that. So probably around 6:00."

"I'll give him a call and ask him to help you."

"Thanks."

I called Wendy. "I'm going to be at Westbrook Mall around 6:00 and possibly tied up there until 7:00 or so at the latest. Have you thought about where to have dinner before going to Brownie's blues club?"

"I'd like to try that new Asian Junction in Old Town; claims to have several vegan options. We could meet there, if you think that would work."

"Sounds good to me. It'll be a straight shot back down Central to Cutter afterwards. Meet up about 7:15 or 7:20?"

"Okay. Are you wearing your Philip Marlowe blue?"

"Yes, why?"

"I'll pick out something to complement it and also bring you a fresh shirt for the evening."

"Great. Oh, if you're wearing heels bring me a pair too. Catch you later."

Five

The Perez-Carrera home was a two-and-a-half-story contemporary probably built in the early '90s and comfortably set back from the street by a well-manicured front lawn. The two-car garage with a room or apartment above was connected to the house via an enclosed breezeway between the room and the house's second story. Isabella Perez-Carrera answered the door and thanked me for coming. She led me to a study/den off the entryway.

"Girls, this is Rachel Cord, the private investigator we hired to help find Maria. Rachel, this is our daughter, Elena, and her and Maria's friends, Taylor Gatwick, Brittany Upchurch, Emily Postern and Lauren Kennedy."

Four of the girls were seated around a table with notebooks and schoolbooks open. Elena, Taylor and Emily were all blue-eyed and blonde, while Brittany had brown eyes and dark hair. Their hairstyles were similar to a Carrie Underwood or Miley Cyrus kind of curly wave. The fifth, Lauren Kennedy, half-sat half-lounged against the arm of an upholstered chair by the windows holding a book. Her brown hair with chestnut undertones was worn straight to just above the shoulder. Her slight nod and half-salute instantly reminded me of a very young, but confident, Lauren Bacall. All the girls wore burgundy sports jackets with the Sacred Heart school crest, white blouses and dark blue-and-white plaid skirts.

Elena bounced up from her seat and came at me demanding, "Have you found my Mia yet?"

"Elena," her mother said. "Where are your manners?"

"Sorry. My apologies, but have you found her?"

"Not yet, but I believe I will find her."

"Good." She turned and returned to her seat next to Taylor.

Brittany and Emily both rose. Brittany gushed forward with hand extended.

"I've never met a real life private detective before. I'm very pleased to meet you. If there's anything we can do to help, we will."

"Thank you."

Taylor whispered in Elena's ear and they both quietly laughed. The movie *Heathers* came to mind—which didn't endear these two to me. I remembered the *Heather* types from my own school past. I didn't particularly want to question the girls together, or with Isabella present, as I'd have to deal with one-upmanship, peer pressure and a probable reluctance to tell me everything I needed to know. I decided on a more neutral beginning.

"It's a pleasure meeting all of you. I do have some questions I'm sure you can help with but don't want to disturb your studies immediately. If I may, Ms. Perez, I'd like to speak with your housekeeper first."

"Certainly. Right this way."

We went out a different door and through a formal dining room to the kitchen where the cooking food smelled delightful.

"Agueda, Miss Cord has some questions about Maria. If you'll excuse me, I have some business I need to finish. Agueda, I'll be in my office."

"*Si, señora.* How may I help you?"

"How long have you worked for the family?"

"For the family, 15 years. For *Señor* Raul and *Señora* Isabella, since they come four years ago."

"So you know Maria quite well?"

"*Si*. She is a very sweet child. She likes to help and learning to cook."

"Any idea why she would run away?"

"No. It is *muy* strange."

"She got along well with her guardians?"

"Of course. What are you thinking? These are very good people. They treat her like daughter."

"Sorry. I didn't mean to suggest otherwise. And Elena?"

"Ah, Elena. My son Fidel calls Elena 'stuck-up.' Sometimes she treat Maria like servant or younger sister she can boss around. Maria just smile and say, '*Si, Elena.*' Then she give me hidden wink. Most times, they get along."

"You and Ms. Perez were having coffee Wednesday morning. Was that here in the kitchen?"

"*Si.*"

"If Maria tried sneaking out at that time, do you think you would have noticed?"

"No. The stairs they are in the entryway and the alarm was off. Her room is at top of stairs. She could sneak out. Why you think she leave?"

"I don't know. That's one of the big questions I'm trying to determine. Thank you for your time."

"*De nada.*"

I went back to the study and leaned against the doorframe. The girls looked up from their work. Lauren had moved from her spot on the upholstered chair to a window seat.

"Would you say that Maria was happy here?"

No one answered immediately, but Emily gave Lauren the briefest of glances. Taylor was the first to speak.

"Duh. Why shouldn't she be happy? She has everything."

"That's what troubles me. Happy people don't usually run away."

"Guess it depends on how you define 'happy,'" Lauren said. Her tilted head, yet direct stare, held an air of amusement. I could definitely see her older self giving that classic lesson on how to whistle.

Elena popped up. "Of course she was happy. She's always been happy."

"Of course, happy people have been known to run off with those they love."

Again, it was Taylor who responded first.

"Maria? Don't be absurd. She still plays with dolls."

"Yes," Elena said. "Ken is the *only* boy she knows."

"And he has no parts," Taylor added. She and Elena both laughed.

"Something you're an expert on," Lauren said. "Parts, that is."

Taylor gave Lauren a nasty stare. "I'm just saying that Maria is still a little girl. Hell, we all know she's not even on the rag yet."

Both Brittany and Emily blushed. Elena, perhaps realizing that the conversation was getting out of hand, said, "If Maria did have an interest in boys, she would tell me first. We have always been close."

"Of course. It was just a thought. Could you show me Maria's room, please?" Elena and I went upstairs. "I suppose Maria being gone changes any weekend plans you have."

"Why? She chose to run away. Why should that ruin my or my friends' Saturday? Some of us haven't finished our Easter shopping."

"Good point. What's a typical Saturday like?"

"Unless there's field hockey or soccer scheduled, it's usually an early matinee movie, lunch and shopping at the mall. No games scheduled because of Easter, so tomorrow it's just fun, fun, fun."

Maria's room was beside the staircase on the second floor as Agueda had said and overlooked the front of the house. It would have been easy for her to sneak down the stairs and leave without being seen. I had the feeling this was probably the smallest of the bedrooms, but it was neat, clean and comfortable. The bed was a three-quarter-sized single with a flowery spread. Window dressings matched. There was a small desk and chair and matching dresser and bookcase. The bookcase held one through six of the Harry Potter books, the *Heralds of Valdemar* series by Mercedes Lackey, Andre Norton's *Witch World* series, the *His Dark Materials* trilogy by Phillip Pullman. Meg Cabot's *The Princess Diaries* books included the newest *Princess on the Brink*. There were books by R. L. Stine and Lemony Snicket, and several 8th Grade school books but no library books.

On the walls were a signed poster from a Cyndi Thomson *My World* concert, a butterfly poster, two drawings of unicorns signed *Maria S.*, and near the door a picture of the Virgin Mary. On top of the dresser and on the desk were ceramic figures of unicorns and butterflies. There was an obvious empty place on the desk.

"Do you know what was here?"

Elena looked over. "A photo of Maria's parents." She turned and looked at the dresser. "There was another of her family and one with me on the dresser, but those are gone too."

"Do you know what else is gone?"

"Her iPod, her blue coat, three pairs of jeans, several Tee shirts, an Aeropostale sweatshirt, at least a dozen underpants and pairs of socks, her Nikes, an American Eagle duffel bag, her missal and rosary, and Julio her stuffed-toy llama. Oh, yes, the backpack that she used for her library books is gone too. The police asked and I helped look."

"You and Taylor said she still played with dolls but I don't see any."

"There was a three-story Barbie house there on the floor. It must be in the attic now."

"How do I get there?"

"That door next to the closet."

The door was locked. "Do you know where the key is?"

Elena opened the closet and reached behind the door jamb. "This is a spare key. The other is with all of the house keys on a ring in mother's office."

I opened the door, flipped a light switch and climbed the stairs. In a well-dusted area near an attic window was Barbie's house with several Barbies and her friends. A picnic cloth was laid out nearby with a tea service set for six. Stuffed animals occupied three of the spots. Closed boxes and light odds-and-ends pieces of furniture filled some of the attic space. I went back down, relocked the door and returned the key to its hook. I looked again at the Cyndi Thomson poster.

I'm not a big Country fan, but the music is prevalent in this part of the heartland so it's hard to ignore. I vaguely recalled that Thomson had been a bright star a few years back who had since faded. But that would have been before Maria came to the States.

"Where did Maria get this poster?"

"I don't remember. Birthday maybe. It showed up some time last year. She really likes that singer. Personally, I prefer Madonna."

"Me too."

I opened desk and dresser drawers and poked under the mattress.

"Does Maria keep a diary?"

"Not that I know —"

Elena was suddenly quiet. I turned to look at her. Her eyes were wide and she was pale.

"Are you okay?"

"Yes, I'm fine. Do you think she had a diary?"

She was glancing around and her brow was furrowed.

"Quite possibly. Many girls do. Don't you?"

"I use MySpace."

"Even for your most personal thoughts and secrets?"

"I don't have—Do you have anything else you need?"

"No, I think we're done here."

Elena hurried downstairs as I followed. She and Taylor were whispering together but stopped when I entered the room. Brittany and Emily were busy working a problem together. Lauren got up from her spot by the window and passed close behind me.

"You sure stuck a bee up her . . . ," she whispered leaving the last word unsaid.

"Elena, I'd like to look at Maria's MySpace account now."

She looked at the computer that sat on a table along one wall.

"You'll have to ask mother. She has Maria's password."

"Where's your mother's office?"

Maria's MySpace consisted mostly of silly backgrounds, photos of family and friends (there was one that included Lauren going parachute off the swings at Radford Park), profile music that included JoJo's *Too Little Too Late*, and messages and emails (most with Emily and Lauren, some with Brittany, only a few with Elena or Taylor, and several with Maria's brother Tomas). Nothing told me where she might be or why she left. I did notice that Elena kept trying to look over her mother's shoulder and was reading what she could as avidly as I was.

Reed Hadley met me at Westbrook Mall. He had one of his staff call up Tuesday night's security footage that was state-of-the-art and stored in computer files; much better than Mr. Bharani's primitive system.

"If your runaway was just meeting someone at the bus stop or changing to the Loop bus and going elsewhere," Hadley said, "our parking lot cameras probably didn't pick her up. We've discussed adding a couple cameras out there, but Corporate hasn't made a decision. It's the old 'chicken/egg' story: spend money now and prevent a possible situation, versus why spend money on something we haven't needed. Anyway, that's not your problem.

"The mall entrance by the Cineplex is the closest to the bus stops. So, if she met someone at the mall or was going to the Cineplex, that's where she most likely entered. That late, she'd need to be accompanied by an adult regardless of the movie rating. Mall policy. So let's see what we got, if anything."

The outside cameras showed most of the pedestrian traffic leaving the mall, not entering. At 8:49 p.m., I thought I saw the girl from Bharani's tape arriving. The computer operator switched to inside cameras so we'd catch her face. It was definitely Maria Salvador. I wasn't particularly surprised that she met Emily, and the girl in the baseball cap was most likely Lauren as all three hugged.

At that moment a male, 18 to early twenties, holding tickets joined them. He and Maria hugged and kissed each other on the cheeks. With his arm around Maria, the four of them entered the theater. Later, as the movies let out, all four came out together and there was clear footage of their faces. Unfortunately, none of the outside cameras caught the vehicle they left in. Hadley provided me date and time-stamped photos from the footage.

"All the girls are supposed to be at the mall tomorrow for a matinee movie, lunch and shopping. I'd like to see if Maria shows up too. Would it be all right if I check in with you again?"

"Not a problem. Bill, make another copy of that photo with

all of their faces for us. I'll have someone monitoring the live footage to catch when they arrive and where they go. We'll set it aside for you if you're not here early enough. Anything else we can do to help?"

"No, I think that'll do it for tonight. Thanks."

So, if Maria sneaked out only to see a movie, why hadn't she returned home? And where were the clothes and other things missing from her room? Why didn't she have the duffel bag or backpack with her? It looked to me as though much of this was definitely preplanned. Most importantly, who was the guy with his arm around Maria?

Six

Wendy and I were running late—something I really hate doing—because service at Asian Junction was slow. Then we got caught in a traffic jam caused by a two-car accident. Brownie had been right about his new singer making his Basement Blues Bistro a success. There were already a few people waiting for the second show or hoping someone left early. Fortunately we didn't need to wait with them. I saw on the marquee that Tristan's name was spelled Sonny and not the Sunny I had assumed.

Sonny was halfway through a smooth Lena Horne version of *Stormy Weather* as we were shown to a booth in the corner where Brownie waited. Listening to her, I was already sorry we missed her opening numbers. A waiter brought me a double Glenfiddich, neat, and a Cosmo for Wendy without being told our order. Brownie had a good memory.

I looked around. The audience was racially mixed: half-black, half everything else. The common denominator being everyone seemed rapt on Sonny Tristan and having a good time. I soon understood why.

Tristan first sang each song in the style of the artist known for that particular song. She emulated Billie Holiday (*All Or Nothing At All*), Ella Fitzgerald (*I've Got Five Dollars*), Etta James (*Something's Got A Hold On Me*), Tina Turner (*Three O'Clock Blues*), Bessie Smith (*'Tain't Nobody's Bizness If I Do*), and many I didn't know like Ida Cox, Ma Rainey and Victoria Spivey. Then she subtly twisted each song on a second run-through until it became hers alone. She could be serious or funny as she played and swayed us with bits of patter between songs and ended with a blues rendition of *Sixteen Tons* I certainly never heard on my mother's stereo.

"Thank you, ladies and gentlemen. We appreciate each of you being here tonight. As we end this half of our show, I'd like to share a song I wrote recently about a low point in my life."

The saxophone introduced her softly as she started out low and smooth, talking asides with the audience, getting nods and smiles in return as the other instruments joined in. As she and the band turned up the volume, they had us laughing, crying, identified and horrified.

I got the Bad Bitch Blues
Said, I got the Bad Bitch Blues
Oh, You know those — Bad Bitch Blues
(Yeah, I see you know what I'm sayin', don't ya, honey?)
Yes, I said the Bad Bitch Blues

And you don't wanna mess
Oh no, you don't wanna mess
You don't never mess with a woman
Got the Bad Bitch Blues

Well, I came home unexpected
An' walked in my door
(I'm talkin' 'bout MY door here. You know: my home, my castle, that private space I pay for.)
When I sniffed musk in the air
(Ooh! Ain't that sweet — my MAN is home.)

Then a whiff of gardenia
Made my nostrils flair.
(Wait a minute. I don't wear gardenia perfume. Who the hell wears—THAT bitch!)

Ooh, I got those Bad Bitch Blues
Suddenly filled with those Bad Bitch Blues
Fumed with those Bad Bitch Blues
Boiled over with those Bad Bitch Blues

And you don't mess with a woman
No, no, don't never mess with a woman
Best stay far from a woman
Got the Bad Bitch Blues

So, I went to my hall closet
Where I keep Daddy's old pump
(That's the shotgun he taught me to shoot when I was just an itty-bitty.)
I jacked in three rounds
And I went on a hunt
(I see ya noddin' back there. You been there, haven't you, honey? Oh, yeah.)

Now, there in my bedroom
(That's my bedroom with the matching dresser, chest and headboard, the flowered spread.)
They was doin' the deed
(You believe that shit? My bed. My clean sheets!)
Ooh, I took steady aim
She saw my gun and I think she peed

Ooh, they got on their knees

47

They begged and they cried
Claimed they wouldn't no more
Said they knew the score
(It was downright embarassing, let me tell you.)
I laid that pump on the floor
Couldn't take any more
Made my way out the door

I was caught by those Bad Bitch Blues
Wanted to wallow in those Bad Bitch Blues
Sink down into those Bad Bitch Blues
Be swallowed by those Bad Bitch Blues

So I found me a bar
I had me three drinks
Thought the mess over
Ordered three Pinks
Went on a stink
'Til I fell on the floor
Stumbled out the door
Went lookin' for a store
To buy me some more

(Yeah, I got wasted for a long while—'bout three years 'fore I got better.)

So don't you mess with a woman
I be tellin' you true
Best not mess with no woman
With the Bad Bitch Blues

Oh, she could be a lover, be a wife

Mother, sister, any woman in your life
And it don't matter her reason
Don't matter her season
There'll just be no pleasin'
If she's got those blues
Those Bad Bitch Blues

Now, she could have a gun
She could have a knife
Better head for the hills, son
Best run for your life

Do you hear what I'm sayin'
Oh, your life would be rife
I mean, what would you do
If she took that knife and she Bobbitts you?

Best listen to me
If you wanna stay free

Don't mess with a woman
I say, don't mess with a woman
'Specially, don't mess with THIS woman
She got the Bad Bitch B-l-u-e-s

You got that straight?

The applause was long and enthusiastic; more than half the crowd standing in appreciation.

"Thank you, all. We're going to take a break, but we'll be back later for another set. If you have to leave, we understand. But if you stick around, it's much appreciated. On drums, please, a big hand for Sandy Thomas; Big Bill Robinson on

49

bass; Light-fingered Darryl Moss at the keyboard; and that mean sax of Carl Setan. I'm Sonny Tristan. Thank you, all. Enjoy."

Before Sonny made it to our table she stopped for autographs several times. A waiter brought us fresh drinks and also set down a glass and filled it from a tall pitcher with iced tea. He left the pitcher on the table. Sonny slid into the booth, emptied the glass in one long swallow and refilled it.

"Oh, boy. I needed that."

"You were great," Wendy said.

"Thank you."

"I agree. How autobiographical was that last song?"

"'Bout fifty-fifty. Never owned a gun of any kind. Tossed a pan of ice water on them. Walked out. Got drunk. Got a divorce. Got drunk again. Stayed drunk. Four years actually; nearly as long as our marriage." Sonny shook her head and held up her glass. "Now it's just iced tea and I can look back and laugh with it."

Brownie made introductions. "Sonny, this is Rachel Cord, the PI I told you about, and Wendy Devlin, her significant other."

"Pleased to meet you. Brownie's told me stories about you."

I glanced at Brownie. "I'll bet he has. He's great for *storytising*. Can I ask why it's Sonny with an 'O' and not a 'U'? I thought 'O's were for boys."

Sonny's face radiated a warm smile, her complexion a lovely *café au lait* in contrast to Brownie's dusky blue-black tones.

"It's a nickname for Sonja with a 'J'. My mother wanted to be a professional ice skater and named me after her childhood idol, Sonja Henie. I think she watched every movie Henie made a hundred times. Car accident stopped mom's plans. While all my friends were getting names like Keisha, Safiya,

Lateefah or Zhenga, I was named for a blonde Norwegian."

"Brownie didn't tell me much on the phone, only that you might need my services, when he asked me to meet you."

Sonny twisted the glass of tea about with her hands. "I'm not sure where to start. You could say it has to do with my song. My ex is here in town and . . ."

"And you don't know if he holds a grudge of some kind?"

"Something like that."

"Has he threatened you or been stalking you?"

"I'm not sure. I've gotten some late night phone calls where no one spoke. I could tell someone was there and then they'd hang up. That's not my ex's style—never knew him to keep his mouth shut—but this started shortly after I heard he'd come to town."

"And this was in her dressing room delivered with a box of rotted funeral flowers."

Brownie passed me a folded piece of paper with *"Sonny"* printed on it in block letters. Inside was a terse note: *"Leaving town is good for one's health."*

"Not very specific. What do the police say?"

Brownie shook his head. "'Bout the same thing. Said they'd speak to the ex, but not much they could do without an actual threat or action. That's why I called you."

"Did you keep the box the flowers were in?"

"Nah. Tossed it and them in the dumpster. They're long gone. Why?"

"Might have been able to track the box to a particular florist. I doubt the rotten flowers came in it, but might have been able to see who bought flowers in that kind of box."

"Didn't think of that. Police didn't ask either."

"What about a restraining order?"

Sonny shook her head. "Had one during the divorce but it expired. Saw no reason to get another. Until now."

"What do you want me to do?"

Brownie tapped the paper laying on the table. "Check out the ex. See if he's the one hasslin' Sonny or not. If not, find who is."

"I don't work cheap."

"I know, but Sonny's fillin' this place every night she appears. Which is good for a new club. She's supposed to stay four more weeks with mutual options for longer. Hate to cut her short. Fact is, I'm hoping she'll want to stay a lot longer. She's makin' this place's reputation. I'll foot the bill."

"Who's the ex and where can I find him?"

"Name's Jacky Fry. Stand-up comic with a three-week gig at Laff-A-Lot out by Cramer College. Thinks he's a Don Rickles clone but less funny in my opinion."

I looked at Sonny. "Anything you can tell me about him?"

"His real name is Joel Freiberg. Don't know if he ever changed it legally. Acts dumb but he's not. Went to some East Coast college and fancy business school I can't recall. He was a CPA for several years before making it as a comic. Taught me how to read spreadsheets and keep books, so I guess I owe him for that. Our marriage wasn't all bad, don't get me wrong. He's . . . he will be 51 this June. I know. Big age difference.

"I was 19 and being offered a record deal, and Jacky was 38 and at the peak of his career, when we met at a party. Got to talking. Thought he was funny, but he had a sweet serious side too. He offered to look at the record contract before I signed as I had a sneaky feeling I was being rushed but couldn't see how. The next day he showed me how. Helped get me a better agent/manager. We started dating. Six weeks later we married. Shouldn't have rushed that, either. I was his fourth wife, after all.

"Anyway, four years, eight months and three weeks down the road, my star was rising and Jacky's was slipping when I caught him in bed with who I thought was my best friend. Found out later she wasn't the first. She found out later she wasn't the last. Like they say, 'leopards don't change their spots.' Hey, like I said, don't get me wrong. Jacky was good to me in many ways. I don't blame him for my being young and foolish and letting his infidelity put me on a drunk spree for as long as it did. That's on me. I just need to know if he's doing this, is all."

I pulled out a business card and pen and wrote my cell number on it before passing it to Sonny.

"If you need anything, call me anytime. If you get another note or package, don't open it. Call me first. Meanwhile, I'll check Fry out but make no promises."

Brownie slipped me a packet of cash along the seat. "Understood. Phil said this would more than cover your usual retainer."

The thickness felt like more than my normal thousand dollars unless he was paying me with ones. I put it in my jacket pocket. We stayed through Sonny's next set. She and her backup group were just as great as the first time. As an encore, they did the *Bad Bitch Blues* a second time, and, again, there were deep groans from the men in the audience when she mentioned being *Bobbitted*.

Seven

Sweat coating me like a second skin trickled between my bare breasts down over my belly. The best part of living in a condo high up overlooking the river was not worrying about peepers when you wanted to lie naked on your balcony and enjoy the late-morning sun.

"Horses sweat," my grandmother's voice in my head corrected me. *"Men perspire. Women glow."*

I looked at Wendy absorbed in a mystery she'd picked up at the library. She definitely glowed. Sunshine glistened her body and sparkled from her moist, deep red, heart-shaped, pubic patch. My fingers lightly brushed my matching pubic mound.

The practice started as a surprise early in our relationship when I got a Brazilian wax and dye job by Barb at Peaches Beauty Therapy. Barb claims the fastest and best Brazilian anywhere and I believe her. So now Wendy and I maintain our red hearts by regular appointments that signal our love — our commitment — more personally than the rings we wear on our right hands.

I breathed longingly as I gazed at her. After two-and-a-half years was I still in lust — as well as love — of this older woman? Oh, yes.

Instead of planning my day's investigative duties, I set aside the titillating Radclyffe I'd been reading hoping to coax

Wendy away from Sheriff Joanna Brady long enough to come sit with me when the doorbell rang.

"Who's that?"

"No idea, but I'll find out.

We weren't expecting anyone. I slipped on my white terry robe and cinched it tight. Through the peep sight I saw a man, mid-30s, wearing brown shorts, a brown short-sleeved shirt and a brown ball cap holding a package and a clipboard.

"Yes? Can I help you?"

"Delivery for Rachel Cord."

"Just a sec."

I slipped the chain, unlocked and opened the door.

"Rachel Cord?"

"Yes."

"Please, sign—"

The man stepped forward, but the clipboard and package were falling to the floor and quickly rising toward my face was the muzzle of a semiautomatic pistol. I instinctively stepped back turning my face away and tried to close the door. The door deflected his hand but the closeness of the muzzle-blast partially blinded and deafened me. I shouldered the door with all of my weight and felt more than heard bones cracking as hand and gun squished between door edge and jamb. I slammed the door with my shoulder again.

I thought I heard screaming. It might have been me yelling, "Bathroom!" or "Phone!" or "911!" Or it could have been Wendy screaming, "Rachel!" Or the man's painful, "Fucking Bitch," as I hit the door again. It's hard to say as my ears were ringing. The gun had fallen inside and I went for it twisting and turning and lying flat on the floor aiming back at the door in a perfect prone position and classic two-handed grip.

The door was partially open and I could blearily see the clipboard and package abandoned in the hallway. My hearing was screwed. I low-crawled to the door, swung it wide and looked out in both directions. The man was gone. I quickly moved to the outside stairwell door, pushed it open and looked down. The man was nearing the bottom of the stairs. I couldn't see the front of the building from where I was. I had no intention of following him—entirely stupid I'm not—but hoped to see which way he went. I propped the door open with a sandal and went down half-a-landing and looked out.

He ran from the building, across the parking lot and around the next building of condos holding his right arm. I hoped he was in a lot of pain. I watched but there was no way to tell which way he went or if he had a vehicle. Nor did I see a UPS truck leave. My vision was clearing as two police cars pulled in with lights flashing. I couldn't hear if their sirens were going or not. I went back to our condo. Wendy was waiting at the door holding the phone.

"You should be locked in the bathroom."

My voice sounded like an echo inside my head. Wendy said something I couldn't understand and touched the left side of my face. It stung and her fingers were smeared with blood.

"I'm okay. It's only muzzle-blast. The police are here. We should go inside. You should put something on."

She said something else. I pointed to my ears.

"Can't really hear you. Go. I'll get a wash cloth for this."

I left the door open, put the gun on the kitchen counter in clear view, wet a clean washcloth, wrapped it around some ice and dabbed at the side of my face. The cloth became speckled with spots of blood. I suddenly felt shaky and weak. Wendy returned wearing sweats as two uniformed police officers came in with guns drawn. They seemed to be yelling, but I still couldn't understand what anyone was saying. Wendy was raising her hands and getting down on the floor. I raised my free hand and knelt also.

Never argue with cops with guns out. They don't know

what happened or could happen. They're just as nervous as anyone. It's best to let them secure the area and then explain. Helps prevent unwanted accidents.

EMTs arrived and treated my face. The damage was a lot less than it could have been: the left half of my face was stippled with partially burned gunpowder and red spots where the powder had drawn blood. I signed a waiver against going to the hospital as nothing seemed to be in my eye, sound was slowly returning, and I promised to see my own doctor as soon as possible.

Shortly later I was sitting at our dining table talking to Det. Sgt. Frank Taylor, an old friend, as his partner, Det. Martin Standish, not so old and not exactly a friend, spoke with Wendy across the room by the balcony glass doors. My ears still rang and I only caught some of Frank's words. He turned my face for a better look at the pattern left from the muzzle-blast. When Forensics arrived they could probably tell me to the millimeter by how much the bullet missed. I didn't really need to know.

"That . . . close."

"Tell me about it. Latest in tattoo design. Think it'll catch on?"

"Not . . . Rachel. . . . could . . . killed. . . . recognize . . . guy?"

"Sorry, but if I don't joke about it I'll probably break down. I've never seen the guy before. Thought he was legit; UPS logo and everything. We're always getting stuff we've ordered online. How'd you get here so quick? It's Saturday."

"On call . . . Charley's."

Charley's Chicago Hot Dog Stand is less than a mile-and-a-half from my condo. Frank claims Charley's as a second home since he left the Windy City. He hates going a day without his hot dog fix even though Lorraine, his wife, had been on him a lot recently about his weight. My guess was that she and the kids were out-of-town.

"Lorraine's parents . . . Branson . . . weekend."

That explained that.

"Tell me . . . happened."

I went through the whole thing again adding bits of detail that came back to me: the guy must have lost his hat on the stairs as I recalled seeing a bald-spot as he ran from the building; he was Caucasian with no discernable accent; 5'8" to 5'10" as I looked at him eye-to-eye and I'm 5'9"; his eyes were brown like his clothes; he was right-handed. I pictured the gun barrel coming up again and shuddered at how close I had come to dying. My mind leaped back nearly three years to when I put my gun to the face of Calvin Tierney who was raping me and pulled the trigger. I shuddered again. That was a dark, haunting memory I had no wish to revisit at the moment, if ever.

"Don't . . . a robbery," Frank said. He pointed first to an evidence baggie that held three shell casings. Then pointed to where the three shots made a hole in one of our balcony window panels and two in the entryway wall beside the kitchen as the closing door pushed the shooter's hand aside.

"Too many shots . . . who . . . you dead?"

"No clue." I tried to play it light. "Maybe Marty there or your buddy Wayne across the river."

Frank didn't find it funny. The truth is private investigators are rarely victims of violent crime despite what novels and movies portray. At least, that's been my overall experience. We're just not worth the time, cost and effort as I see it. We fill a needed niche in an over-populated, but under-staffed and under-paid society. We find people, for various purposes; track people, for various purposes; check backgrounds, stories, alibis, do research and investigate possible wrongdoing. We're nosy parkers by nature, and although "private investigator" sounds exotic and exciting, it's often boring and, basically, we're just data processors.

Which didn't change the fact that someone just tried to kill me. Had he gone for a body shot first instead of my face, I most probably *would* be dead. So—who? Why?

"Looks personal . . . sure you . . . know who?"

Though I only heard that first shot that went off in my face, I had to agree that three rapidly fired shots seemed pretty personal to me too.

"No one comes to mind. Normally, I don't get blamed for what an investigation reveals; that's usually reserved for the lawyers and clients."

"How 'bout relatives of . . . like Tierney . . . Archer? Maybe Barrow?"

"Don't know. Maybe." I had personally killed Tierney and Gwen Archer. "No one's ever made threats. It's been three years. If it's because of them, why now? Vincent Barrow pled out and is upstate doing 10-to-14. Doesn't seem like his style. Sorry, Frank. Can't get my head around the idea that someone wants me dead. Have to think on it."

"'Sallright. Take . . . time. You still . . . guns . . . office?"

I nodded.

"Might want . . . till . . . catch this guy."

I nodded agreement.

As we waited for Forensics to arrive, Standish left to coordinate a search for witnesses, a listing of all vehicles still parked in the area to check out, and the locations of security cameras. Frank phoned in a description of the suspect and his probable injuries for a BOLO and a checking of area hospitals and clinics, including those across the river. I wanted to shower and get dressed, but Frank made me wait.

"Forensics needs to . . . you for evidence, too."

Neatly bagged on the table were the clipboard, the package, the man's hat recovered from the stairwell and the gun. The hat had what looked to me like an official UPS logo. The gun was a compact Taurus PT 24/7 9mm easily held and hidden by the clipboard.

"Frank, I never touched the trigger. Any prints are definitely his."

"Best bet's gonna . . . clipboard, maybe the package or . . . magazine and bullets . . . DNA . . . hatband . . . doorjamb. Don't play with . . . evidence."

I put down the baggie with the shell casings and looked across the room at the hole in our window. I couldn't get over how quickly the guy had fired three shots. My sight drifted to where I thought it and the others might have gone had I not deflected his hand and he had still missed me. Where had Wendy been sitting or had she gotten up?

My mind took another backward leap. I saw Henry Seiko, the man who had killed my lover Karen Tanaka and several other American-Japanese women, holding a knife and threatening Wendy. Saw again her pulling away, the knife slashing, me shooting him, Wendy on the floor the knife in her side. Another dark memory not to be dwelled upon; but how not to at this moment? Someone trying to kill me had endangered Wendy too.

Frank slapped my hand and I released the baggie, again. To reduce temptation, we moved to sit near Wendy in the living room. Thinking of how close she too came to being hurt, I wanted to hold her, comfort her, but didn't. Frank hadn't said anything, but I understood he wouldn't want Wendy or I touching before Forensics arrived. Wendy would be swabbed for evidence also. I knew that Frank believed our versions of what happened, but also knew that he wasn't going to let some later defense lawyer make an argument of sloppy evidence gathering because of friendship and overlooking the possibility that this was just a domestic incident between two dykes.

My hearing improved and to pass time Frank updated me on recent changes with people we knew. Detectives Ed Montero and Kerri Trujillo both passed the lieutenant's exams and been promoted. Kerri was now in charge of the city's Sex

Crimes Division where she had worked for several years. Montero was transferred back to this district and was Frank's boss. Dean Lockhart, Montero's old partner, was still at Central Division and breaking in a new partner. I asked Frank how he liked working for Montero.

Frank smiled. "Better him than some others who wanted the job. At least Ed's a real cop, not one of those pencil pushers who came up through Admin."

"Why'd you never take the test?"

"Too much paperwork. I spend too long at a desk now with just my reports. Taking care of Standish and myself is job enough. The extra grade and bump in pay aren't worth it to me. 'Sides, I retire in a couple more years."

Once Forensics arrived, things went quickly: they swabbed Wendy and me—which meant we could touch and hold each other again— then dusted, gathered, measured and photographed, took trajectories, cut holes in the wall to recover bullets, even sent a team out with a metal detector on the possibility that the bullet that went through our window glass fell short of the river. As they were wrapping up, one of the Forensics people took Frank aside. He came back to the couch.

"You sure the guy wasn't wearing gloves?"

"Quite sure. Why?"

"No prints on the clipboard or the package or on the stairway banister where we found fresh blood."

"What's that mean?" Wendy asked.

"That this guy's a pro or a very careful, determined amateur. Either way, I don't think Rachel's seen the last of him."

Wendy squeezed my hand.

Eight

After Frank and the others left, I got to hold Wendy and try to calm us both. The idea that I was in someone's crosshairs was nervewracking. Still, I had things that needed doing. I headed for the shower.

In the shower I tried to think of who would want me dead. Were there relatives of Gwen Archer and Calvin Tierney looking for my blood? What about Archer's partners, Carl Cheswick and John Thornton? They lost everything when the child pornography and killings came to light. Cheswick even lost his home paying for his defense. They beat the porn and child killing charges but were sent to federal prison on money laundering and conspiracy convictions. Were they still in prison or not? Did they hold a grudge worth killing over and hired someone to do it? Who else could there be? I had no answers.

Little of the stippling came off in the shower. I didn't have time for a masque and peel. I'd do that later. I used a heavier than usual foundation to cover the stippling as best I could. As I came out of the bedroom wearing a Cramer College sweatshirt, jeans and cross-trainers, my hair in a ponytail, Wendy looked at me in surprise.

"Where are you going?"

"First to the office to pick up guns and then to Westbrook Mall. Despite what happened here, I've still a runaway teen to find."

"How can you be so glib about what just happened? Someone just shot at you and could have killed you. Aren't you afraid he'll try again?"

"Very much so. I'm afraid for you too. Afraid of you being hurt inadvertently. We need to protect ourselves. That's why I'm going to get guns first. I'll drop one here for you. Don't give me that look. I know you don't like guns, but sometimes they're necessary."

"It's not just a dislike. I hate them. I hate the necessity of them. I don't know why I let you teach me to use one or how you talked me into getting a carry permit."

"You were recovering. You were vulnerable. But seeing you stabbed nearly broke my heart. I swore I wouldn't let it happen again. That's why I taught you to defend yourself, why the permit. As for now, that bullet that missed me could just as easily have hit you. The hole in our window proves that."

Wendy put her arms around me. "I'm afraid. Stay here. Please."

"I want to. Believe me. I know you're afraid. I am too. But I've also got a job I'm being paid to do. I think I can find Maria soon. Possibly today. There are things I don't understand about her disappearance. Things that don't add up; don't mesh in my head. I'm hoping for answers today."

"Don't you care how terrified I am? What if he comes back?"

"Of course I care. It's not that. Look, the guy's hurt; needs medical attention. So I don't think he'll try again today. Besides, Frank said there'd be a patrol car sitting in the parking lot just in case. Though we can't count on that long term. So we have to protect ourselves. No, I don't think the creep will be back until he heals or devises another plan. Maybe I'm wrong, but I can't just sit around and wait for that to happen."

"Staying with me isn't just sitting around."

"Of course it's not. That's not what I meant."

"It's just . . ."

"Just what?"

"I don't know."

I kissed her softly.

"I don't know, either. I don't know who this guy is or why he hates me, but I agree with Frank this is personal. So we aren't taking chances. You *will* have a gun available. What you do with it is up to you. I realize that. I taught you to use it. I can't make you do it."

"Okay. I just don't want you to go. I don't want to be alone."

"I know, but I think there's a good chance I'll find Maria today. I really need to go."

We held tightly for several moments. Wendy's hands reached under my sweatshirt and her nails scratched a pleasurable line up my spine. Her lips nuzzled my ear. She softly whispered.

"Fuck. I can't believe what I'm thinking right this moment. What I'm feeling. Are you sure your search can't wait a little longer? Hmmmm?"

Wendy's hand slid around to my front and fondled my breast. Teased my nipple. Mmmmmm.

I could have told Wendy—maybe should have told Wendy—that that intense sexual desire she suddenly felt was a normal relief feeling of being alive after a near death experience, as multiple therapists have reminded me. Innumerable people—especially soldiers and police—have suffered that particular guilt trip which often leads to PTSD, alcoholism, drug addition or worse.

There's a hair's breadth difference between guilt and acceptance when you play the coulda-shoulda-woulda game after a traumatic event. The thing is we all do it, consciously or not. Every action — or no action — has consequences as Newton taught us.

My first realization of that came during the First Gulf War with the Scud missile attack on our barracks in Dhahran, Saudi Arabia. It killed 27 reservists, wounded nearly 100 others including a friend who traded MP patrol duties with me. It should have been me — not her — getting hurt that night instead of my enjoying the sexual embrace of another woman. I felt guilty for that for several years.

The thing is I had no more control of where that missile came down than the people who fired it. My friend could still have been injured or been among the dead that night even if I'd gone on patrol. Another instance is when I was tortured and raped and had to kill two people to save myself. I should have had backup — could have had backup — instead of going it alone. But the situation I walked into was not what I expected. Continued guilt for things beyond my control, or for past mistakes, has always been a problem for me. It's something I'll probably always have to deal with.

That's what I could have or should have said instead of relishing Wendy's embrace. Then again, why waste the moment — I had wanted her earlier, after all.

I redressed and was out the door only an hour or so behind schedule. Hadley said his team would be on the lookout for my runaway, so it didn't matter that much that I was a bit late.

Nine

Arriving at **Westbrook Mall,** I went first to security where they let me review that morning's activities. Right on time, my gaggle of girls had arrived in a black limo and went into the Cineplex-14 to catch the matinee. However, a few minutes later Elena, Taylor and Brittany went back out the entrance and got into a white SUV waiting at the curb and were driven away. That was unexpected.

I asked to see previous Saturdays' video files. Two other times in the past month it was the same routine except that only Elena and Taylor left in the SUV. A review showed them coming back each time around 4:00 p.m. and meeting their friends—including Maria—at the food court where they talked and went through purchases from various stores splitting up the bags. What was going on? Was this part of my missing puzzle?

Lauren and Emily could still be at the movies or may be out and about the mall. Mall security missed seeing them again on any of the video cameras after they all arrived. They were still checking and had a couple of people out doing walkthroughs at various stores. Was Maria here, too? If so, no camera had picked her out yet.

I decided to go walkabout and ended half-an-hour later at the food court sipping a latté and studying the madding parade around me. Hoping to see one of my threesome.

A couple tables away were a father and daughter who had been shopping at the Gap. The man was clean cut, early-30s, wearing a polo shirt and slacks; the girl wore faded ripped jeans and an oversized football jersey. She wore too much mascara trying to look 15 or 16 or older, but the way she enjoyed her Happy Meal made me wonder if she were any older than 12. Was this a divorced dad spending time—?

A booming voice caught my attention and everyone else's.

"Hey, Big Daddy! What are you doing pimping here?"

Tiger Lil, from the Lillith Society, strode across the court and right up to the twosome I'd been watching. She pulled out a chair and made herself to home.

"You rewarding your new whore or are you still grooming this one?"

The man spoke quietly but I was close enough to hear the conversation.

"Shut your yap and get out of here before I call security."

Lil smiled but was no quieter than she had been. "Oh, yes, by all means, let's call security. I want to see you explain your relationship to this obvious tweenager."

The man's right hand slipped into his pocket and came out holding a switchblade below the table. I started to get up. Lil saw my action and recognized me. She shook her head slightly so I resettled into my seat. The guy saw Lil's reaction and looked over his shoulder. I pointed to his hand and shook my finger back-and-forth as if to say, "that's a no-no." His hand went back in his pocket and came out empty. Lil had turned her attention to the girl with whom she spoke more quietly.

"Hi, I'm Lil. Has this man touched you inappropriately yet or is he still pretending to be Mr. Nice?"

The girl seemed confused and didn't answer; the man leaned forward saying something I couldn't hear. Lil raised her voice.

"Of course this concerns me! And every other decent person! You're scum, Big Daddy! You put little girls on the street to have sex to support you. You should be locked away never to be seen or heard from again."

The man stood. Half the people in the food court were now watching. The back of his neck was deep red; his clenched hands were white at the knuckles.

"Let's go, Joy."

"The girl stays here."

The man's hand started for his pocket again, but another woman and three teenaged girls suddenly appeared beside Lil. He looked around and saw how visible he was. He obviously didn't want a scene. He turned and walked quickly away. The girls and woman pulled over extra chairs, sat, and began talking to Joy. Lil got up and came to my table.

"Hi, Rachel. Sorry for the disturbance."

"Not a problem. Looks like you had everything under control. What's the story?"

"Same old, same old. Just the faces change. Though it does seem like they're getting younger every day."

Originally from here, Tiger Lil was an ex-prostitute who had run away and started tricking in New York City at 14. At 18, she met Rachel Lloyd the founder of Girls Educational and Mentoring Services. With Lloyd's help and others at GEMS, Lil broke from her life, got her GED, and graduated with a combined B.A./M.A. degree in Psychology from City College of New York. She returned home two years ago and founded The Lillith Society based on the vision and mission of GEMS to end the commercial sexual exploitation and trafficking of children and to empower girls and young women to exit the commercial sex industry. On her blouse was a button that said, "Girls are not for sale."

"This girl was seen at the bus station yesterday talking to Big Daddy. Someone let us know they were here today. Think we've saved this one in time. By the way, I saw your email about your runaway. None of my people have seen her. Have you found her yet?"

"I've got a good lead I'm following up. If I'm right—"

My cell phone rang. I glanced at the screen. It was Frank Taylor.

"I need to take this."

"Good luck with your runaway. Catch you later."

"Thanks, Lil. You too. Hey, Frank. Tell me you caught my shooter already."

"We caught your shooter already."

"Really? Who is he?"

"I'm not being serious. Of course we haven't caught him or have any idea who he is. Who do you think we are, one of those TV cop shows with 16 commercial breaks and the case is solved in under an hour?"

"Okay. Okay. Point taken. Why are you calling?"

"Just to say that no one's shown up yet at any emergency room with a busted-up right hand. We're still checking private clinics though. The main thing is, Forensics found bits of glue on the gun's grip. We think the guy coated his fingers and palms with glue and that's why no prints yet you saw no gloves."

"Don't like the sound of that."

"Nor do we. This guy's careful. Even the bullets and magazine were wiped clean."

"DNA results?"

Frank was silent.

"Sorry. You're not TV cops, I know. Maybe next week if we're lucky, right?"

"Try next month if you win the lottery. Budgets rule and lab requests just keep stacking. It's not like you were actually shot or are anyone important like the president or governor or even one of us lowly civil servants."

"Right. Any good news?"

"Guy's blood type is O positive."

"Oh, great. That really narrows it down."

We both laughed. Nearly 40 percent of the population is O positive. I mentioned Cheswick and Thornton as remote possibilies and he said he'd check them out.

"Anything else, Frank?"

"Yeah, where are you?"

"Westbrook Mall, why?"

"Because you should be home—"

"Frank, I can't hide. That's not me. Besides, the guy's hurt and not coming after me again today. And I've got a 13-year-old to find."

"That may be true but you've a very scared woman at home too."

"Did Wendy call you?"

"No. I happened to call there first."

"What'd she say?"

"It's not so much what she said, as how she said it and what she didn't say."

"She should be fine. The door's locked and she won't let anyone in; she has 911 on speed dial; and, she's got my backup gun."

"Right. A gun she's used—what? Maybe half-a-dozen times on paper targets in three years? What she needs is you."

"Frank—"

"Did I ever tell you why we moved here from Chicago?"

"Just that Lorraine needed to be here to care for an ill family member, and that there was a detective opening here you could get."

"That's only half the story. I worked a lot of undercover back there and I was good at it. I lived for my job, but didn't see the effect it had on my family. We nearly separated.

Robbery/Homicide has its dangers like every cop job, but nothing like I faced daily back then. Moving saved my marriage and probably an ulcer or two.

"Frank—"

"I'm just saying, take it from a long-married man and listen to your woman. Not just the words but what she's really saying."

"Okay . . . Thanks."

Maybe Frank was right. Maybe I was tone deaf to Wendy's feelings and thoughts. How much of that lovemaking session before I left was due to the adrenaline rush of just being alive; how much to worry and fear; how much to love and passion? I felt a throbbing and warmth start between my legs. Not now. Not now.

I looked over at the other table, but Tiger Lil and the others were gone. I scanned the area again but didn't see anyone who looked like Maria, Emily or Lauren. I started another walk around the mall.

Ten

"**M**iss Cord?"

I stopped and turned. Emily Postern came out of the Aeropostale store.

"Hi, Emily."

"I thought that was you, but you're dressed so differently."

"It's Saturday. Can I help you?"

"I . . ." She looked around. "That is . . . Have you found Maria yet?"

"Not yet. Do you know where she is?"

Her eyes widened and she looked off to the side.

"How would I know where she is?"

How indeed?

"Is there something you'd like to tell me or ask?"

"Ah . . ."

"There's a place over there we can sit if you'd like."

"Okay."

The bench was out of the traffic where I could still watch people passing as well as keep an eye on Aeropostale. I wanted to see who was with Emily. See who else might come out of the store. She set her two shopping bags on the ground next to her feet. She nervously played with her hair. It was obvious she wanted to say something, but she kept hesitating.

I waited for her to speak. It was best not to lead her and was often the best way to get information.

Finally, she blurted, "Are you a lesbian?"

"What? Am I—"

"I'm sorry, I shouldn't have—"

"No, no. That's quite all right. I just wasn't expecting that particular question."

"I really am sorry. The way you were dressed yesterday, I wondered, and if you . . ."

"It's really okay. Yes, I'm lesbian. Why?"

"I was wondering . . . that is . . . how . . . when . . .?"

"How and when I knew?"

She nodded.

"That's harder to answer. Is your interest mere curiosity or are you trying to sort out your own thoughts?"

"Well . . ."

"Let me put it this way: I can only speak for myself. Every person's life and experience is their own. Growing up on a farm in rural Iowa, I knew about the birds and bees as well as cattle, horses, pigs and goats at a very young age. Overhearing the jokes and innuendo of older brothers' conversations, and a 6th-grade class on human reproduction, I had a fair idea of human sex too. Not that same-sex attraction was discussed or thought about. It wasn't.

"My personal sexual awareness didn't occur until much later with my best friend—another girl. That's not unusual for either gender, but I didn't know that at the time. We were 15 that first time; later than most, I guess. Can't say I gave sex a whole lot of thought back then. I did date some boys in high school, but it was only with my friend that things felt right. By the time I graduated high school, I had no doubt which way I was bent sexually, but as to the exact how and when moment I have no idea."

Emily stared at the ground not saying anything.

"If you're starting to experience sexual feelings and attraction toward someone you know, you're perfectly normal. Happens to everyone. Gender doesn't matter. It doesn't mean you're lesbian or not, or will be or not. Just that you're moving into a new phase of growing up."

"So when will I know?"

"Can't tell you that, sorry. Like most things in the real world, life's a crapshoot. We don't know the result until after we roll the dice."

"Doesn't seem fair."

"Things rarely are — fair, that is."

A few minutes passed with no one saying anything. I kept my eyes on the entrance to Aeropostale.

"Why do you think Maria ran away?"

Emily looked at me. "I . . . wouldn't know."

"Of course you wouldn't. How was the movie Tuesday night? Did you see *Meet the Robinsons* or *The Last Mimzy?*"

I turned to look at her. Her mouth was gaping. I smiled then went back to watching the entrance to Aeropostale.

"How . . .?"

"Mall security cameras."

She sighed in resignation. "The *Bridge to Terebithia*. It was sad, but we liked it."

"I would have bet on *The Last Mimzy*. Who was the adult guy with you? Is he why Maria ran away?"

Lauren came out of Aeropostale carrying four bags. She looked around. I waved. She came over.

"She knows about Maria Tuesday night."

Lauren cocked her head and looked at me.

"Join us."

Lauren sat next to Emily and gave her hand a reassuring squeeze.

"So, who wants to go first? No takers? Okay, I'll start. Maria is hiding at . . ."

Neither girl spoke but I was willing to wait.

"Mouse's."

"Thank you, Lauren. That wasn't so hard, now was it? Emily, are your parents involved? Do they know?"

"Mouse's parents are divorced. Her mom is away on business and Em's staying with her dad right now. There's no one at her house."

"What about the guy from the other night?"

"My brother Charles."

"What's his involvement?"

"None. He joined the Marines and left for boot camp Wednesday morning. He wanted to treat me to a going away thing, so I asked if I could invite Mouse and Maria to a movie. He didn't know Maria was running away. After the movie, he dropped us at Em's."

"Okay. Now, my big question: Why? Come on. This is not the time for reticence. I can't help if I don't know what's going on."

"Elena. Elena's been pressuring Maria to do something she shouldn't, and Maria's been . . . She doesn't want to get Elena in trouble and keep her from staying here."

"Staying here? I thought the family was returning to Peru."

"They are, but Elena might stay with her cousins when they come and get to finish school here. Possibly even stay for college. Maria too."

"So Maria isn't being abused or anything at home?"

"Good God, no. Just browbeaten and overlorded by Elena. Sometimes I think Elena treats her like a slave. Usually Maria capitulates or ignores it. This time, she didn't know what to do. So she ran away."

"What's the *something* Elena wants Maria to do? Come on,

full story. Trust me, I've heard it all."

"Elena and Taylor have been selling drugs—just marijuana—to other kids at school."

"And they want Maria to help sell them?"

"No. Help get more to sell."

"Is this connected with the SUV they got into this morning?"

"How do you know about that?"

"Security cameras. All of you were seen arriving for the movies, and then Elena, Taylor and Brittany left and got into a white SUV. Were they going to buy drugs?"

Lauren shook her head. "They don't buy them; they trade for them."

"Trade what?"

Lauren hesitated for several moments.

"Trade? What?"

Lauren blushed. "BJs."

"BJs? Do you mean blowjobs? Are you telling me they trade sex for drugs?"

"Taylor says BJs aren't real sex. Only—"

"Let's not have a semantic war as to what sex is or isn't. I don't suppose Sacred Heart teaches about STDs and condoms, do they?"

"Just abstinence and marriage. Taylor says you only get diseases through real sex outside of marriage."

"Ah, yes. The all-knowing Taylor. Was this her idea?"

"Don't know. She and Elena presented it together."

"I suppose Taylor wouldn't call what they're doing prostitution either, would she?"

"Of course not! They don't do this for cash."

"No, they do it for marijuana which they then sell for cash. Think it through and then explain to me the difference."

Neither girl had an answer. From the looks on their faces

the truth may have been sinking in.

"Do you know how much they get paid — excuse me — trade per BJ?"

"Taylor says never less than five joints. That's they're bottom line. Elena said she once got 10 joints. I think they average seven."

"Ready-made joints or bulk that Taylor and Elena put together later."

"Ready-made. They don't want to be bothered with production."

"Of course not. How much do they sell the joints for at school?"

"Three dollars each for grape; $5 each for cherry. Discounts if you buy three or more at a time."

"Grape and cherry?"

"The marijuana is mixed with grape- or cherry-flavored tobacco. Supposedly the cherry has a higher grade marijuana."

"Who's supplying them?"

"Some college guys at Cramer."

"How's business?"

"They sell out every week they get a supply."

"How many joints are we talking about?"

"Sixty to 80 depending on flavor."

"That's a hell of a lot of BJs."

"Said they could sell twice as much which is why Elena was pressuring Maria."

"Why Maria? As Taylor so crudely put it yesterday, Maria hasn't started puberty yet. Why not you?"

"I already turned them down. Mouse too. As for Maria, Elena has always been able to get Maria to do her bidding. Just not this time. Now that Brittany's joined them, they hope to increase their supply."

"Brittany hasn't done this before?"

"No. Today's her first time. You may have noticed that Brit is a Taylor and Elena wannabe. When Maria ran away, Brit volunteered."

"How long has this been going on?"

"Before Thanksgiving. Taylor and Elena said it'd be an easy way to get money for Christmas."

"Is that when Maria's grades started slipping?"

"Yes. She was so happy when she started homeschooling. Thought Elena would leave her alone after that, but that didn't happen."

"Okay. Let me guess. While Elena and Taylor—and now Brittany—are off sucking joints for joints, the rest of you watch a movie and shop for yourselves and them. Then you all meet up later, fill them in on details of the film and any unusual happenings here at the mall should anyone ask. Then you all go home together, right? And for this cover, you're cut is what?"

"Ten dollars each, plus the price of the movie and snacks. Lunch too."

"You do realize what you're doing is against the law, right?"

"Taylor says we're not hurting—"

"Lauren, stop with the 'Taylor says' business."

"What do you mean?"

"Yesterday you had no problem contradicting or standing up to Taylor. Does she do your thinking? Is she your master?"

"No way."

"Then don't use her or Elena as justification for your actions."

"I suppose we're busted."

"Emily, please don't cry."

"We're going to jail, aren't we? My mom will kill me."

"Not necessarily. Let's not get ahead of ourselves. Right now, Maria needs your help. I need your help. Here's a tissue. Let me think a moment. It's 3:35. Lauren, when are you supposed to meet up?"

"Usually around 4:00 at the food court. Taylor's dad's chauffeur is our ride today, and we're to meet him out front at 5:00."

"Not much time. Come with me."

"Where are we going?"

"My car. I want to see the drop-off, but I don't want Elena or Taylor to know about this conversation. Relax. I'll explain in the car."

At the car, I got my camera kit out and set up with a zoom lens. Lauren sat in front with me; Emily was in back with the shopping bags. I moved the car to a better view of the mall entrance near the Cineplex-14.

"Here's the drill. I was hired to find Maria and bring her home safely. I'm not a cop and I'm not anyone's moral compass. Elena's and Taylor's enterprise is not a priority other than how it affects my bringing Maria home.

"As I see it, Brittany's volunteering relieves the pressure on Maria for now—possibly permanently. Maria should be able to go home, but your and Emily's involvement in hiding her could cause problems which I'm also sure Maria would not want. So the three of you need a cover story. I think I can provide that. I'll need to make some calls and contacts to work out details. Are you seeing Maria tonight?"

"Yes. Mouse's dad thinks she's spending the weekend at my house, and my parents think I'm going to be at her dad's. We're really going to be with Maria at Mouse's."

"Good. What time?"

"Not later than 6:30."

"Okay. Do you have cell phones? Write the numbers here for me. I'll meet you at Emily's around 7:00, no later than 7:30.

I'll call first and even bring pizza. Anyone like anchovies? Me, neither."

"Can you really get us out of this?"

"I'll do what I can. You'll have to trust me."

"Can we? Trust you, that is?"

"Do you have a choice?" Lauren shook her head. "This may be our car now. Once the girls go in, you and Emily follow and meet up as planned. Try to be natural."

I focused my lens on the white SUV taking several shots of the car and driver. I got shots of Elena, Taylor and Brittany getting out making sure that I included the vehicle and its license tag. On close-up, Brittany looked like she was one step from tears but was bravely smiling. Elena and Taylor were laughing at something the driver may have said. My lip-reading ability is not that great but I'd swear that Taylor said, "I bet you will," as she ran her tongue across her lips. The threesome entered the mall.

"Okay, go. See you tonight."

I watched Lauren and Emily enter the building. I hoped Emily wouldn't fall apart. My clients' interests are important to me, but I always strive to consider the welfare of the child at all times. Sometimes that causes conflicts. Fortunately, that didn't seem to be an issue here but there were complexities to deal with. I also don't like lying to children or breaking laws when I can avoid it. I meant it when I told Lauren I would do the best I could.

Had this scheme involved 18-year-olds, I wouldn't like it, but I wouldn't make an issue of it, either. Adults, even young naïve ones, can make their own choices and live with the consequences. I'll admit I'm also wishy-washy on sex involving 15-to-17-year-olds as I'd hate to be hypocritical about my own past. However, these girls were 13 and the guys involved were all adults. I could not allow this situation to continue.

The SUV was at the exit waiting for a break in traffic. I

pulled up behind and then followed. Near Cramer College the SUV pulled into a lot and the driver went into a Piggly Wiggly.

Shortly later, the driver I'd been following returned with two cases of beer, several bags of chips and I don't know what else. He looked like a typical Cramer student in his early 20s. I took more pictures and followed along. He turned down Greek Avenue but went past all of the fraternities and sororities turning at last onto a side street away from campus. He pulled into a private drive, parked and went in the front of a large two-story house. Four other vehicles were parked there too. I took pictures of those and what tags I could see and wrote out the address and time; then drove back to Piggly Wiggly.

After using the bathroom and buying a diet soda and bear claw, I called PJs in Lincoln Heights.

"PJs, Shoshana speaking."

"Hey, Shoshana. Didn't expect you to answer. It's Rachel Cord."

"Where else would I be for Easter but Grandma's? It's really good to hear your voice. Did you get the invites to Rasheena's and my graduations?"

"I did. Congratulations to both of you. They're attached to my fridge and marked in my calendar."

"Thank you. If you're calling about that girl you emailed us yesterday, Grandma says she hasn't seen her."

"It is about her, but I've already found her and plan to take her home in the morning."

"Great. Is she okay?"

"As far as I know at the moment, she is. However, for reasons I can't go into right now, I need to alibi her whereabouts for Wednesday morning through tonight. She's done nothing illegal and I don't really expect anyone to ask; I just need to say she was somewhere she wasn't."

"I gotcha. Maria Sandoval? I'm sorry, I meant to say Salvador. Yes, she was here. One of our girls, can't recall which one right now, found her crying at the bus depot Wednesday and brought her here. Oh, she was no trouble at all. What does she like, again?"

"She very into Harry Potter."

"That's right. She knows everything about Harry Potter. Talked for hours. Got to practice my Spanish. We had a great time. Rachel Cord came and talked with her and took her home Easter morning."

"Thanks. That'll do it."

"No problem. I'll pass the word to Grandma and mama. Tell us about it someday."

"Will do."

"And as Grandma and mama say, don't be a stranger."

"Promise not to. Thanks, again."

That covered, I called mall security and thanked them for their assistance, and that I had a solid lead on my runaway's whereabouts. I asked them to save me the footage of the girls getting in and out of the white SUV on several Saturdays. I'd come in Monday morning to look it over and get some photos for my final report if that was all right.

I didn't say anything about the sex/drug angle or my developing plan to stop that. They did ask about the loud argument in the food court I witnessed. They couldn't get anyone to the scene quickly enough before it broke up, although they had it on video. Witness statements they did get were conflicting and unhelpful. I filled them in on what happened and they planned to make "Big Daddy" permanently *persona non grata*.

I headed home.

Eleven

"That's disgusting! Thirteen-year-olds? I know that you were only hired to *find* this girl and I don't *care* whose idea it was, but you can *not* let it continue."

"I don't intend to, but first I need to get Maria home. And to do that successfully, I need her cooperation. I'm going to try and do that this evening. Hopefully, I'll take her home without any backlash tomorrow morning. Then I'll deal with the sex for weed problem."

Wendy's anger over what the girls had been up to made her forget just how scared she'd been earlier. That was a plus for me. She held up some earrings to see if those were what she wanted to wear. She turned to me.

"I can't believe how stupid these girls are."

"Naïve and pampered may be closer to reality, but as Forrest would have said, 'Stupid is as stupid does.'"

"Makes me mad enough to shoot someone."

"I agree. Speaking of which, did Frank fill you in on the guy who shot at us?"

"Just that they hadn't found him, and that he wanted to talk to you. Any idea who he is?"

"Not yet. No fingerprints to check against, and it could be weeks before DNA results are available."

"Weeks?"

"If we're lucky. Budgets rule as Frank says. There's just never enough money for everything. The lab's way backed up on testing. Frank said it could take even longer as we're low priority."

"Low priority?"

"Two scared women who peed their pants is way down the list from someone actually shot or a death or—heaven forbid—someone with real clout like a politician."

"I don't recall either of us wearing pants at the time."

"You know what I meant."

"It's ridiculous. What do we pay taxes for?"

"General welfare and common defense. You about ready?"

"Yes. Do you realize how long it's been since we went out two nights in a row?"

"No. Which means it's been way too long. Sorry."

"No need for 'Sorry;' I've been remiss too."

As we left the condo, Wendy stopped to stare at the shooter's bloodstain still on the doorjamb.

"Sorry about that. I'll clean it off when we get back."

Wendy shook her head. "No. Leave it. I'll take care of it."

At her insistence, I dropped Wendy at Belle's Diner with her Jance mystery, picked up pizzas at Mama Rosa's and met the three girls at Emily's. I felt good that I had read these girls correctly and that Maria hadn't disappeared again.

I kept the conversation light at first, and off the subject of going home, by getting them to talk about Harry Potter. As the woman at the library had said, Maria really came alive on the subject. Not only was her English excellent, but she was quite adept at accents as well. I hadn't read the books, and only seen the first film, but an online search had given me enough background to keep up my end of the conversation.

I knew that fans identified with Hogwart's school houses and wasn't surprised that Emily and Maria belonged to Hufflepuff or that Lauren was Ravenclaw. We all burst out laughing when I asked where they placed Elena and Taylor, and the instant answer from all of us was Slitherin.

As the laughing died the tone in the room changed becoming quite quiet. Maria looked at me. There was a forlornness in her gaze, but also a quiet resolve.

"I should go home, shouldn't I?"

"Unless you've come up with a better plan, it seems like the right answer to me."

"Running away seemed like a good idea. Now I don't know."

"The Perez-Carreras care for you a lot."

"I know. They've been good to me. The *señora* and *señor* were childhood friends with my parents, as are Elena and I. Do you know this?" I shook my head. "Our families have been connected for generations. Even so, the Perezes and the Carreras are a small part of our population who trace their families to the conquistadors and before that to pre-Moorish Spain. They take great pride of having never mixed with others. The Malfoys in Harry Potter are like this. They mistakenly believe this purity makes them superior. Elena, at her worst, is like this too."

"And Taylor?"

"She thinks she's superior because her family has lots of money and buys her what she wants when she wants it. She's just spoiled. Another Malfoy trait."

Maria looked at her two friends and then back at me.

"Lauren says you have a plan that won't get them in trouble. Is this true?"

I told her of the alibi I set up to hide Emily's and Lauren's involvement in her running away. Of her supposed conversations with Shoshana and PJs.

"What should I say about why I left?"

"I've tried thinking of something elaborate, but the simple classic teenage line, 'I don't know,' may work best. Isabella and Raul will be glad that you're back and safe, and that they don't have to tell your parents you're missing."

"And Elena?"

"She's not going to say anything to her parents. If she bugs you—which I doubt—just look her straight in the eye and say, 'you know why.' She won't pursue it. She's a manipulative little . . . witch, but she's not dumb. Might even be nicer to you until she thinks it's blown over."

Maria was quiet for several minutes.

"I'd like to go home now, please."

"You sure?"

"Yes. Tomorrow's Easter. It will make *Señora* Isabella happy that we are all together at morning Mass."

While the girls packed Maria's things in her duffel, I called PJs' and gave them the slight change in alibi should it ever be needed; called Isabella to say that I found Maria and was bringing her home; and then called Wendy. Wendy said to take whatever time I needed; she was enjoying her book, the pie and coffee at Belle's were excellent, and that they served a vegan-acceptable veggie burger so we could eat there when I did arrive.

Twelve

I'm not overly fond of "insult artists" who claim to be comedians, as I find no humor in their so-called "jokes." And while "hate" or "disgust" may be extreme that's probably closer to my true feelings. Perhaps "dull" is the safest description. And Jacky Fry had to be among the dullest as well as, I would say, least attractive. He's the last person I'd have pictured Sonny living with—much less actually marrying. Maybe he had more hair and less fat back then.

"Hey, folks. I'd like to say you've been a wonderful audience. You weren't, so I won't. Though you have left me full of wonder.

"Like, I wonder why you laughed at jokes three and four but not five. Or at seven, eight or nine, either. Whatsamatter? No sense of humor? These jokes were funny. Some cost me as much as five bucks. So, what is it? You all part of a proctology convention?

"Yeah, makes me wonder. I wonder why the guy at the table here kept checking his watch like he had an appointment but stayed for the whole show. Your date stand you up? Can happen to the best of us—or in your case, the least.

Yeah, I wonder. I wonder why that lady in the back hides her face whenever someone comes in. Hey, lady, isn't that your husband next to you?

"And these two sweethearts over here. I wonder why these

guys kept their hands under the table all night. Hey! This is a family place. Get a room somewhere.

"Yeah, I wonder. Wonder why you're all sitting here 'stead of somewhere else. Whatever the reason, the management and I appreciate it.

"But, I *especially* appreciate this lady here on my right. She must be from Texas, folks. 'Cause as everyone knows, everything's *BIG* in Texas. Makes me want to udder those immoral words of Bob Hope, *Thanks for the mammaries* . . . And thanks to all of you for coming tonight. If the *BIG* lady would like to join me in back, I'll come too.

"Catch ya all later. Oh, yeah, one final word from my sponsor, the management: buy more drinks or get outta here."

The lights came up slightly and an emcee came out.

"How about another round of applause for that international comedic star Jacky Fry? And remember, you can catch more of Jacky exclusively here at the Laff-A-Lot through April 21st. As an added bonus, Jacky will be one of our 'Open Mike Nite' judges this coming Wednesday and again on the 18th. Don't miss what should be some exciting evenings of blistering comedic evaluations. But stick around as we have more for you tonight starting with last week's Open Mike winners Steve Goldman and Krystal Young after this short intermission."

Wendy stifled a yawn. "Are we having fun yet?"

"Just getting started. Time to go backstage."

"Why?"

"Two reasons: one, to see if fat, bald and stupid is really behind Sonny's harassment, and, two, because we were invited."

"I think you were the one invited, and I've seen what you can do with a magazine."

Wendy pointed to the several copies of the club's monthly program I had unconsciously rolled into a tight cylinder about a finger's width in diameter. Tightly rolled paper has great strength and makes an effective and unobtrusive weapon. With enough force, it can damage internal organs—possibly fatally. Unrolled it reverts to its newspaper, magazine or—as in this case—program innocent self. I shrugged and headed for the area behind the stage. Wendy followed. A large man blocked our path.

"Sorry, only staff and invited guests are allowed backstage."

I hadn't dressed the part, but I let Charlotte's deep syrupy southern voice take over as I pulled my shoulders back to enhance my bosom. "But suh, didn't you heah Jacky invite me backstage a moment ago?"

He mulled it over as he gazed at me, then smiled. "You're right, he did. Fourth on the left. Name's on the door."

"Thank you so much."

As we neared the door, we could hear arguing but it was difficult to pick out whole sentences or tell who was saying what: "don't need cops hassling" "fuckin' stupid" "fired" "you can't fire" "Try me" "Oughta kill . . ." I knocked on the door. The man who answered was mid-40s with dark hair and eyes wearing a decently fitted gray suit. He glanced at the rolled up programs I was holding.

"We are heah to see Jacky."

"Sorry, ladies. Mr. Fry isn't giving out autographs tonight."

"But he invited us to join him."

"Who is it?"

"A couple women from the audience."

"Well show 'em in. Don't be a killjoy as well as a schmuck."

"Thank you for seeing us, Mr. Fry. I'm Rachel, and this is Wendy. Remember us?"

"Well, well, well. Can't say the faces are familiar, but I'll never forget those bazooms. It's my BIG lady from Texas."

"I'm not really from Texas, Mr. Fry."

"Doesn't matter. Just bring your gorgeous beauties over here and have a seat on my lap. We can have a drink and talk about the first thing that comes up."

Wendy's hand on my wrist restrained me from doing what I was thinking.

"Aren't you going to introduce us to your friend?"

"That's not my friend. That's my so-called manager, Judas Finkman. He's just leaving — permanently."

"Jacky's idea of a joke. The name is Brinkman, Ron Brinkman."

"How do you do?"

"Get lost, Judas. The river's east of here. Find a short pier for a long walk, will ya?"

"Goodnight, ladies. We'll talk tomorrow, Jacky."

"Over your dead body. And not before. Get the fuck outta here!"

Brinkman left the room closing the door behind him.

"Now, where were we? Oh, yeah. I don't know what bazooms cost these days, but someone got more than his money's worth."

"No one paid for these, Mr. Fry. They're home grown."

"Even better. But my father is Mr. Fry, call me Jacky."

I dropped the affected accent. "Actually, your father is Benjamin Freiberg of Erie, Pennsylvania."

"If you know that, then I'm guessing you weren't here just to see my show."

"That's very perceptive. Here's my card. I'm a private investigator."

"The way you're stacked, you're your own honey trap. So who you working for? The current Mrs. F or one of the leeches who thinks I still owe her something?"

"Sonny Tristan."

"That fucking Brinkman. The cops hassled me about that already. That's why I'm pissed at Brinkman. Believe me, it won't happen again."

"You're saying Brinkman sent the threats and you didn't know about it? Why'd he do it?"

"That new song of hers: *The Bad Bitch Blues.* He heard a record producer liked it and was going to offer her an album. Thought it'd come out it was about me and that it'd hurt my bookings. And his percentage. As if negative publicity ever hurt a comic like me. The putz."

"So Sonny has nothing to worry about now?"

"Just being the star she should've been years ago. She spent too much of her life on our break-up. Wish her well for me, will ya? And remind her to read the fine print before signing anything."

"Will do. Thank you for seeing us, Mr. Fry."

"Yeah, sure. Why don't you stick around? We could have some laughs and drinks."

"Already have a date, thanks. Goodnight, Mr. Fry."

"Hey, before you leave. What'd you think of the show?"

"Bob Newhart you're not."

"Everyone's a critic. Get outta here."

Thirteen

All in all, Easter was a quiet day. Wendy and I slept late, had an at-home brunch and an early dinner with Clare, who was not only Wendy's mother but was one of my survivor sisters.

Like the others in the group I belonged to, Clare had been raped. She was also the eldest victim. She was 70 when it happened and was left in a field to live or die.

I was far from the youngest in the group, but at the time I joined I was the newest victim. It was to these women that I first shared the details of my ordeal, fully faced what had happened, and truly realized I was not alone in the world. It was through their strengths and courage and support that I found that I could not only live with what had happened, but that I could take control of it and stop being the victim.

The group grows and shrinks, but like caring sisters, we all stay in contact should any one of us need help getting through a period of depression or unwanted remembrance. It was through Clare that I met Wendy.

I did try contacting Sonny Easter morning to give her some peace of mind but her cell phone was off; I left a message. I tried again later in the day with the same result. I did reach Brownie and updated him and said I'd be returning most of what he'd given me. I didn't feel I'd really earned anything.

There was no news on my would-be murderer which was

good in a way. It let us relax enough to spend the rest of Sunday with Wendy finishing her Sheriff Brady mystery and starting another J. A. Jance novel featuring someone named Ali Reynolds while I did Internet searches. I did not tell Wendy I was looking for possible porn images of my favorite Sacred Heart sweeties, Elena and Taylor. She was upset enough about that whole situation.

I couldn't be sure, but given the college-aged guys involved, the proliferation of digital cameras—even cell phones had them now—and the anonymity aspect of the Internet, there was a good probability that the girls were somewhere online whether they knew it or not.

Resetting my search engine's filter to "SafeSearch off" and using various keywords, I quickly—less than a second—had tens of millions of images of penises and young girls' faces. Further filtering brought that number down significantly to mere thousands and had me looking at uploads coming mostly from my city.

Several hours of boring searching later, there they were. The site claimed that all participants were at least 18, but "Sandy and Mandy" definitely weren't. Somewhat surprising was that in many of the photos the males were as identifiable as my two sweethearts, as well as there being enough background to specify the rooms where the pictures were taken. I printed several screen shots and made note of the site's web address.

I've never understood the appeal of having sex with children. I recognize that it exists, but don't understand the mind set. Like Wendy, I find it repugnant. The guys in the photos took advantage of the girls' naïveté about trading drugs for sex, but they also exploited them by taking pictures and posting them online. Elena and Taylor were stupid, but they didn't deserve that.

Common sense kept me from doing what I wanted to do. Which was to go find those guys and shoot their cocks off. I'd let the Law do it instead.

Ethan Fletcher.

God! Where did that come from? I hadn't thought of Fletcher in . . . what? More than 10 years, at least. Why now? Was it because he was court-martialed for having sex with a minor? Because I testified against him? He wasn't the guy that tried to kill me, but could he be the reason behind it? Is that why his name popped into my head. Damn. That was so long ago. Surely, he couldn't be . . .

A quick online search didn't bring up anything on the Ethan Fletcher I once knew. Nor did a more thorough hunt at *IRBsearch*. I wasn't completely surprised. Fletcher's crime occurred in Germany and before the first sex offenders registries began. Still, there should be something on him somewhere. Just the routine stuff, if nothing else. He couldn't have just fallen off the face of the earth.

Fletcher and I served in the same MP unit in Germany, in '92. It was my next—and last—assignment after returning stateside from Desert Shield/Desert Storm. We weren't the best of friends or even that close, but being in the same unit meant being brother and sister in a way. That's the way the military is. You try to look after each other. Overall, he was a good soldier. Just that one fuck up.

It was the beginning of carnival season. Octoberfest was in high gear. Anyone not on duty was partying somewhere, whether it was downtown, or at one of the big clubs at the American community across town, or just the local one on post.

That Saturday night, I and a few friends were at our local club. It was crowded due to the rare appearance of a live band. The band was four, young, American guys on drums, keyboard, bass and lead guitar. As I recall, they were just high school kids from across town but they had a good sound. They mostly did covers of a lot of bands like Queen, the Stones, Aerosmith, Kansas, America and the like with a few of their own songs thrown in. The crowd was enthusiastic and roared when they played *We Are The Champions* and *A Horse With No Name*, but I particularly liked their version of *Dust In The Wind*.

My current girlfriend kept nudging me under the table with her knee. I knew she wanted to head back to the barracks for some hot action. I was having a good time and tried to ignore her temptations. Besides, I figured the longer I delayed our departure, the hornier she'd be.

There was a lot of dancing going on, and across the room one particular girl stood out. I thought she looked a bit young but couldn't be sure. I was sure, though, that she was a civilian. Probably a date, maybe even a wife, of some soldier. She was having a great time and danced with anyone and nearly everyone. It was that kind of night. I would have danced with her too, if I hadn't been with my girlfriend, or — more likely — too worried about publicly outing myself. There were some things you just didn't do back then. Being discreet was my MO as I had no desire to get thrown out before my ETS.

After another hour or so and several beers, I let my hand wander into my girlfriend's crotch just to let her know it was time to go. I felt her heat. Yep. Definitely time to go.

Getting near our barracks, a street light partially lit an alleyway between buildings. I glanced over and saw two people having sex. They were in a tight embrace. The woman was supported against the wall with her bare legs wrapped around the guy's middle. His pants down around his knees. I pointed them out to my girlfriend, and we watched for just a moment. We had no intention to stand and stare; we had our own orgy to go to.

Just then, the woman saw us and began screaming, "Rape!" There was nothing we could do at that point but put a stop to what was happening. The woman turned out to be the girl from the club, and the guy was Ethan Fletcher. In the half-light of the alleyway, with her hair mussed, her blouse and skirt wrinkled and her undies lying on the ground, the girl suddenly looked younger than she had at the club. Someone else must have heard her scream, because moments later a roving patrol showed up. The four of us were taken to the MP station for questioning and statements. Instead of cuddling with my girlfriend, I spent the night talking to a sergeant with CID.

It turned out that the girl's father was an Air Force major at the nearby Air base, and she went to the same high school as the band members. She and a few other girls had been guests of the band. The worst thing was she was only 15. Though I swear, and 50 others at the club that night did too, that she looked more like 18 or 19. She even had fake ID that said so. Fletcher claimed the sex was consenual. None of that made any difference at his Special court-martial. She was 15, he was over 21. Case closed.

I remember once overhearing one of my brothers telling a friend to stay away from jailbait because "15 will get you 20." Fortunately, for Ethan Fletcher, he only got two years at the U.S. Confinement Facility in Mannheim, reduction to E-1, and a Bad Conduct Discharge. As for the girl, she never had to appear in court. Her father was suddenly reassigned stateside, and he and his entire family were on a plane within three days of the incident.

It was a rotten deal all around. The girl shouldn't have been there. The club staff should have caught the fake ID and not served her drinks. Fletcher should have been more attuned to her true age instead of being drunk and horny. Hell, we were all drunk and horny that night. I often wondered if we hadn't stopped to look, if the girl would have hollered rape or not. I never came to an adequate answer. The result was a good soldier going to jail, an Air Force major losing a plum assignment, a family disrupted, and a young girl's innocence torn asunder. Such a waste.

So where was Fletcher now? Did he hold a grudge? I didn't have time to worry if Fletcher was behind the attempt on my life. I had no way to locate him or connect the dots. So it didn't really matter. I had bigger concerns at the moment.

There were other girls now whose innocence was gone forever; whose lives and families would probably be disrupted further by my actions. But the situation couldn't go on. Whether or not Elena and Taylor instigated the whole thing, the guys that used them were more responsible. They had to be put away. For a long time, I hoped. I finished putting together my packet of evidence and made plans for the next day.

Fourteen

Early Monday I went back to the house near Cramer College and set up my camera. I took several photos of guys leaving for classes or wherever. I was pleased to recognize two guys from my online search. By 10:00 a.m., the only vehicle left at the house was the white SUV I followed Saturday, so I headed for Westbrook Mall to pick up the photos I needed from their security footage.

I thought I had enough of a package to give Kerri Trujillo for her to get probable search and arrest warrants. I hoped that would lead to the end of Elena's and Taylor's enterprise without compromising Maria, Emily and Lauren. That was a lot of hoping. It would depend a great deal on how cooperative Kerri might be. Also on how things went down.

I phoned Kerri to congratulate her on her promotion and asked her to lunch as well as to discuss what I had in mind. She agreed to meet unofficially downtown at 1:30 at Preston's Restaurant near her office. I went home and printed the rest of the photos I needed for the packet to give Kerri.

I arrived at Preston's early, managed a window table as a group was leaving and ordered coffee while I waited. My phone rang. There was no name, but the first three digits gave the impression the call was coming from Police Central, CPD headquarters only around the corner. Maybe Kerri was running late. I answered.

"Ms. Cord, this is Detective Dean Lockhart from Central Division. It's been a couple years since we last met so I don't know if you remember—"

"I remember you quite well, detective. You were partnered with Ed Montero. How can I help you?"

"I have some questions I'm hoping you can answer."

Questions? I could think of nothing I had going or recently been involved with that would interest Lockhart.

"Certainly, if I can. What are they?"

"Call me old-fashioned, but I'd prefer to meet in person. Are you available this afternoon?"

I prefer face-to-face interviews also so I can read expressions and body language; but before submitting me to Lockhart's scrutiny and questions, I wanted more information, if I could get it.

"I've an appointment in a few minutes but should be free after 3:00 p.m. However, meeting is going to require one of us traveling to the other's location." Like all of two blocks at the moment. "Unless your questions are quite complex, I see no reason for either of us to be inconvenienced or you delayed in getting your answers. I presume this involves something you're working on, so ask away."

A brief hesitancy and a feeling of exasperation came across, as if he'd just lost an opening round, before Lockhart asked his questions. Then again, it could just be my projecting my feelings had our roles been reversed.

"Could you tell me where you were yesterday?"

"That's a pretty broad timeframe, and I have no idea why you're asking, but I'm sure you'll enlighten me eventually. Basically from shortly after midnight Saturday until about 6:30 this morning, I was either at home or at a friend's for Easter dinner."

"Can anyone verify that for me?"

Why would he need verification?

"My partner. She was with me the entire time."

"Partner?"

"That's partner as in the person I live with, not as in business partner. My business is still a one-woman shop. My partner is Wendy Devlin, a VP at First National Trust & Savings. We had dinner at her mother's home. That's Ms. Clare Devlin. Here are their numbers. Now, may I ask why you want to know?"

"Do you know Ronald Brinkman?"

Fry's manager?

"I was briefly introduced to a Ron Brinkman Saturday night."

"Where and when exactly?"

"Backstage at the Laff-A-Lot comedy club around 11:00 p.m. He's agent/manager for comedian Jacky Fry who's appearing there. We were introduced and then he left."

"Was he with anyone?"

"Just Mr. Fry in the dressing room. He left alone."

"And you didn't see him again after that?"

"No."

"Are Brinkman or Fry clients of yours?"

Hardly. Where are we going with this?

"No. Wendy and I were in the audience and Fry invited us backstage after the show."

"Why did he do that? Did you know him?"

"We'd never met. Maybe he liked the way we laughed at his jokes." Or didn't.

"Did you give Brinkman one of your business cards?"

Were we getting to the point at last?

"I did not. Why are you asking?"

"Do you have any idea where Brinkman would get your card?"

This was worse than pulling hen's teeth.

"Have you asked Brinkman?"

"That's not possible. Again, Ms. Cord, I think it would be better to continue this in person. If you could—"

Did Brinkman have one of my cards? If so, why wouldn't or couldn't he say where he got it? Why was it important to a detective in Robbery/Homicide? I glanced out the window and saw Kerri waiting for the light to change so she could cross the street. I interrupted Lockhart.

"I agree, detective, we should meet. I've been in business nine years and I've given out thousands of cards. My appointment is arriving so I really can't speculate on where Brinkman got one at the moment. However, as I said, I should be free by 3:00. I could meet you by 3:30—depending upon traffic and parking, of course—at your office if that would help."

"I wouldn't want to inconvenience you. I could be at your office by 3:00, and if you're still busy I don't mind waiting."

"Actually, I'm not at my office and won't be, so it would be more convenient for me to come to you."

"Fine. I'll be expecting you."

So much for that. Lockhart didn't seem any happier than I did, but at least *he* knew why he wanted the information. Had Brinkman done something yesterday, or had something happened to Brinkman? Did it involve Sonny Tristan in any way? Had he tried to harass her again? According to Fry, Brinkman was responsible for harassing Sonny already. Yet he also said that was taken care of. Was it? What was Lockhart's interest?

Brinkman wasn't talking but obviously he had one of my cards. Where did he get it? I could think of three possibilities. One—the least likely—was random chance. Two, the card I gave Fry. Did he give it to Brinkman later? Three, the card I gave Sonny. Did she confront Brinkman? How did she find out about him? I hadn't been able to reach her to give her the information I got from Fry. I was getting a bad feeling. If something happened involving Brinkman, I liked possibility three the least.

Fifteen

I **turned my phone off** as I didn't want more interruptions. Kerri Trujillo looked good for a mother with four kids and as the head of an entire police section.

"Congratulations, again, on your promotion. How's it feel to be the boss lady?"

"I've been the 'boss lady' quite a while but finally getting the rank and pay that goes with it is great. How you doing?"

"Quite well, overall. Business is steady and I've put away enough to get these downsized to normal, if not modest. Deconstruction is next month."

"Then congratulations to both of us. Speaking of next month, do you remember Kayla Barnes?"

"Sure. I get Christmas cards from her and her mother. Kayla's home in Colorado; going to be a senior this year at Colorado College. Why?"

"We caught her rapists. Most of them anyway."

"It's been nearly three years. When? How?"

"DNA. Picked up a grad student on a date-rape charge at Cramer. Compared his DNA to outstanding cases and came back with a positive match for Kayla's case. He and his lawyer are cutting a deal with the DA. He's already outed three others and we picked them up. Two of them are DNA matches as well, and the third admitted to it saying he used a condom. He could prove our best witness. Claims it's haunted him all this time and he's glad it's out. Didn't haunt him enough to come forward sooner though. Asshole. Still, he's given us more names. We're processing warrants now."

"That's great. Does Kayla know?"

"Spoke with her and her mother this morning. She sounds relieved. Thought you'd like to know too."

"Thanks. So how many we talking about? As I recall, there were four DNA specimens."

"Five DNAs. Looks like six, maybe eight, assholes were involved. It was a huge party that night, hundreds of people, no real supervision. Kayla was knocked out on roofies in an upstairs bedroom, door open to anyone who wanted a piece. My regretful asshole says he and another guy felt badly enough to dress her and put her on the patio where you found her."

"Will she need to testify?"

"Hard to say. Up to the DA, but I doubt it. She was heavily drugged at the time and didn't know it was happening. She won't have much testimony to give, but a jury would like to see her stand up anyway. On the plus side, we have two cooperating participants willing to make deals. Others could flip too. So this may never go to trial. I'm really hoping at least one of these guys can finger the bastard that slipped the drugs into her drink to begin with. Meanwhile, I'm rushing to pick up everyone involved and get indictments before we run into statute of limitation issues."

"Why? There's no statute of limitation on rape in this state."

"True, but from what I've heard so far, a couple of the guys just jacked-off on her face. No penetration. Ergo, no rape. Still, I'd like to pin everyone I can with some kind of sexual assault felony, if possible, or at least get their arrests into the public record. Gotta get it done this month before I hit that three-year wall. None of these guys deserve a bye in my book."

"Good luck with that. Which, in a way, brings me to what I wanted to see you about."

"I knew there was something you wanted besides taking me to lunch. Can we order first, though? This is the first lunch in weeks that wasn't at my desk."

We ordered our food and I gave Kerri the packet I'd put together. As we ate, she went through the material looking at the photos and the notes I'd written out as I gave her the rundown. She shook her head.

"Sacred Heart. This is so hard to believe. My two oldest girls go there. My youngest starts kindergarten there this fall. You sure about these girls' ages?"

"Positive. I interviewed them this past week while looking for a runaway. These girls are classmates. One of the reasons the girl ran away was she was being pressured by these two to help with their sex for pot barter scheme."

"So how would you like me to handle it?"

"An anonymous tip? Then your people can verify it with your own research and follow through from there. Once I found the girl, I sort of promised I'd try not to get anyone into too much trouble so that she'd go home. But I can't let these guys get away with sexually exploiting children no matter whose idea this may have been."

The waitress was headed our way so I covered the photos with the envelope.

"Will there be anything else?"

Kerri said, "coffee and two servings of your triple-chocolate cake, please. We're celebrating. That and the check should do it."

"Be right back with your dessert."

When the waitress left, Kerri put everything back in the envelope.

"With what you've given me, I could have warrants today

and bust this place with an early morning wake-up tomorrow. But . . ."

"But it would be better if you catch them with the girls there."

"Right. I don't need to catch them in the act; these photos and what my people will download from the Internet will establish that. Finding the girls at the scene seals it tight and should have the guys wanting to deal without facing a public trial. That may save these girls and their families from some public humiliation. It might also keep your involvement out of it, and that of those you're trying to protect. But I can't make any promises or guarantees. You say this goes on every Saturday?"

"Not necessarily, but as often as the girls can manage it is my understanding."

"Next Saturday?"

"Highly probable, but I can't be certain. I am certain it'll continue until it's stopped, though."

"Do you think these two girls really thought this up on their own?"

"They're bright. They're imaginative. It's possible. I think *they* believe they thought it up. But they're also very young. I think someone planted the seed of an idea and let it grow on its own. I also doubt that this is a one-shot deal. It's too simple an idea. There could be other girls at other schools doing the same thing. Be surprised if something like this isn't happening across the country."

"That's a very cynical attitude."

"I know. I hate to think it could be true, but it is suspicious. If someone had the time and resources to follow it up . . ."

"Who's got that kind of budget?"

"I don't know. Homeland Security? I mean, if this isn't as big a threat to the country's wellbeing as a terrorist attack, what is? It's not like the information isn't available. Security cameras are going up everywhere. Regular people are starting to post pictures and videos online to social sites every day. It's just a matter of writing software to look for what you want to find and follow it back to the source."

"Big Brother is watching."

"Something like that. Welcome to the fishbowl. Scary stuff, huh?"

"When it was science fiction it was scary. This is downright piss your pants frightening."

On that high note we finished our cake and coffee, I paid the check, left a generous tip, and we walked out into our not so brave new world view.

Sixteen

Detective Dean Lockhart looked up from his desk at my smiling face. He nodded to the officer who escorted me upstairs.

"You're much earlier than I expected."

"I had no problems with traffic and finding parking was a piece of cake."

"Well, thank you for coming in. Have a seat."

"Always happy to help the police."

Lockhart's right eyebrow raised a smidge.

"So, how can I help you now?"

"Ronald Brinkman. Are you sure you've never met with him before or after Saturday night at the Laff-A-Lot?"

"If he's the same man I met in Mr. Fry's dressing room, I'm quite sure."

"Do you know where he's staying?"

"No. But if I were trying to locate him, I'd start with the three-star hotels."

"Why is that?"

"The way he looked when we met. His gray suit fitted him well and was of good quality. Conservative blue tie. No ostentatious jewelry. Styled haircut. Shined shoes. Can't picture him in a motel or hotel of lesser quality unless that's all that's available. But he's a businessman and will want to keep costs down. My guess is that he wants some amenities but wouldn't see value in the price of five-star dazzle. For his top or up-and-coming clients, sure; not for himself though. I think he'd opt for a four-star if the price were right."

"How about the Downtown Marriott?"

"Lots of good restaurants and bars in the area to meet and greet clients; easy to get around. Yeah, I could see that — if he got a good discount."

"Any likelihood he'd pick up your card at the Marriott?"

"Remote possibility, I guess. I've never stayed there or interviewed anyone there. There are several law firms and businesses downtown where I've left cards in the past. And I've done numerous interviews in the area leaving my card for follow-up info. It might help if I knew which printing he has. I've made changes over the years." In other words, show me what you've got.

Lockhart looked down at his desk, shook his head, opened a drawer. Had I won another round? He handed me an evidence baggie with one of my business cards inside. I didn't bother trying to memorize or decipher the case number on the outside, the baggie alone told me Lockhart was ready to tell me any bad news. As for the card, it was from my most recent printing. I had changed the font size and placement of the address and phone number. All in all it's a nice card on quality cardstock. Clean, crisp, black lettering. Engraved, not raised. No fancy embellishments or logos. I turned the baggie over to look at the back. I was glad to see that it wasn't the card I had given Sonny.

"This is my newest card. Here's another for comparison. I'd say there aren't more than a hundred and fifty of these scattered around the city. Definitely less than two hundred. I couldn't say where Brinkman got his, but I did give one to Fry later that night."

"Why was that?"

"What I do came up in conversation so I gave him a card."

"But Fry is not a client, right?"

"That's correct. You ready to tell me what happened to Brinkman?"

"What makes you think anything happened to him?"

"You asking questions, my card in an evidence baggie with a case number, and Brinkman not saying where he got it."

"Ronald Brinkman is dead."

Worst-case scenario. "Sorry to hear that. How did he die?"

"Why are you sorry? You said you only met him briefly."

"I'm always sorry to hear of a death. As John Donne said, 'each man's death diminishes me.' So again I ask, how did he die?"

"Yet to be determined."

"But suspicious, right?"

"What makes you say that?"

"Again, you. You wouldn't be asking questions if his death wasn't suspicious. Call it the 'Nosy Parker' part of my personality. It's why I do what I do."

"And why we do what we do. Right now we're gathering facts and information without speculating outcome. So, do you have anything that could enlighten us one way or another?"

I wasn't sure how to answer. As I had told him, I was sorry for Brinkman's death, but I wished Lockhart were more forthcoming. It was obvious Brinkman died sometime between when I saw him and when Lockhart called me. Probably at the Marriott. Lockhart was awaiting answers as to how and why. My not being totally candid about seeing Fry could be a problem. I could try justifying myself that "I had answered his questions" all I wanted, but I knew that wouldn't fly in the long run. Especially if it turned out Brinkman hadn't died of natural causes or by sheer accident. Yet I was worried that I hadn't heard from Sonny and didn't know where she had been Sunday.

Lockhart put the evidence baggie in his drawer and leaned back in his chair.

"Ms. Cord. We don't have a relationship like you do with some others in the department, but have *I* ever treated you with less than respect and candor?"

"No."

"Then please extend me the same courtesy."

Lockhart was right. He'd always treated previous interviews in a neutral, unbiased, nonjudgmental way. He let evidence lead him to conclusions, rather than forcing evidence to support particular theories as others have done. I had no reason to make his job harder or be obstructive.

I apologized and told him a client had received implied threats that may have come from Fry, which was why I went to see his show and speak with him. Fry claimed Brinkman made the threats without his knowlege, and that he put a stop to them. I also said I heard Fry make what might be considered threats to Brinkman. But wouldn't be able to swear to that interpretation.

"It's possible, though, that the card you have is the one I gave Fry."

"So it's possible Fry saw Brinkman again after you spoke with him."

"I suppose it's possible. He didn't indicate he was going to, though."

"Does your client know that Brinkman was the source of the threats?"

"I don't know. I haven't spoken with her since my talk with Fry."

"Why is that?"

"Her phone has been off, and she hasn't returned my messages."

"Could this card be the one you gave your client?"

"No. I wrote additional phone numbers on that card so she

could reach me at any time."

"But she hasn't called you?"

"No. As I said, I haven't spoken with her since talking with Fry."

"Do you know where your client was Sunday, or where I can find her now?"

"No. We haven't been in contact as I've said."

"What's your client's name?"

There was no point in not telling him. Sonny and Brownie had made an official complaint, and Lockhart would find out one way or another anyway.

"Sonny Tristan. She's currently appearing at the Basement Blues Bistro on Cutter Avenue."

"What's her address and phone number?"

"I only have her cell phone number. I'll write it down for you."

"Thank you. If I have more questions, or have information I *can* share, I'll let you know. When you do speak with your client, please let me know. I need to see her. I'll get someone to show you out. One last thing. Please don't mention Brinkman's death to anyone. I haven't confirmed that next of kin has been notified."

Seventeen

I **turned my phone on** to try Sonny again and found a message from Frank Taylor. As much as I wanted to know what Frank wanted, I tried Sonny first. Again, all I got was voice mail. It worried me that I couldn't reach her, and I wanted to know where she'd been Sunday. I left another message to call me immediately; then I called Frank.

"Hey, Frank, Rachel. Any good news?"

"Certainly hope so. The Regional Trauma Center for Washington County treated a farm worker for a smashed right hand Saturday evening. That's about 50 or 60 miles from here. The worker claimed his hand got caught when a horse kicked a stall door closed on him. The guy fits the description we put out. The sheriff over there has sent out a couple deputies to check out the guy and his story. I'm waiting for a callback."

"Did you get a name?"

"Claude Akins. We've got nothing in the system by that name. Mean anything to you?"

"Not really, but it sounds familiar. Have to think on it. Anything else?"

"Nope. Just wanted you to know you're not forgotten. Will let you know when I have something."

"Thanks, Frank."

Why would a farm worker from Washington County want

to kill me? I couldn't recall working any cases down that way, and yet the name Claude Akins seemed awfully familiar. A gravelly voice and rugged features fuzzily rose from memory. I hoped the sheriff called back soon with answers. Sheriff? Had Frank mentioned the sheriff's name? Was it Lobo? Why Sheriff Lobo? Damn!

It was remotely possible someone in Washington County tried to shoot me, but I doubted he was at whatever farm address he gave the medical people. And I knew damn well his name wouldn't be that of actor Claude Akins. I highly doubted he was going to get caught this easily. Just have to stay alert to what was happening around me.

I called Brownie and asked if he'd heard anything from Sonny.

"Nah. I tried calling her yesterday after you and I spoke but only got voice mail. Left messages but nothing back yet. After Saturday's shows, she said she was going to spend Easter with an aunt and cousins across the river. We're closed today so I expect she's still there. She and the band will be here in the morning at 9:00 to do a run-through for tomorrow night's show. I'll see her then. Is there anything wrong? Should I be worried?"

"Not that I'm aware of. Just wanted to speak to her directly that she had nothing to worry about from Fry and that the harassment would stop. Do you have the address of where she's staying?"

"She's at the Southside Inn & Suites on South River Drive. Not that far from where you live."

I drove to the Southside Inn & Suites. As Brownie said, it was only a few blocks south of my condo. I checked with management but Sonny wasn't in. I left another message for her to call. I also called Lockhart to give him Sonny's address. He thanked me but said he'd already gotten it from Brownie.

Around 7:00 p.m., I heard from Lockhart again.

"Have you spoken with your client or Jacky Fry since we

talked?"

"No, why?"

"I haven't been able to contact either of them. If you hear anything, please let me know immediately, if you will."

"Sure."

"And, again, please don't mention Brinkman's death to anyone."

"Haven't said anything about it, nor do I plan to. G'night."

Where was Sonny? Was she involved in Brinkman's death? What about Jacky Fry? Had he carried out his threat?

Eighteen

There was the briefest of stories in the morning *Daily Record* that a guest of the Marriot had been found dead in his room Monday. No details were given and the name was still being withheld.

I met Brownie at the club and gave him his retainer back less two hundred to cover my time and expenses. The band was setting up and tuning their instruments, but Sonny hadn't arrived. Brownie tried reaching her, but her cell was still off, and she didn't answer the phone at her hotel suite. No one in the band had heard from her either.

At 10:45, just as we were getting seriously worried, Sonny rushed in. She apologized for being late. Said she overslept and that traffic was backed up coming across the river from her aunt's place. She seemed nervous and distracted, and the run-through wasn't much of a success. Sonny said she'd be fine by show time. About all that was accomplished was deciding which songs they'd be doing later that night.

I didn't call Lockhart while they were rehearsing. I needed to know where she was when Brinkman died, first. I offered to buy her lunch hoping she wanted to talk.

"There's a great hot dog place just a couple of blocks from here, or for more variety I can recommend Phil's Tearoom."

Sonny said she'd like that. She was hungry as she'd skipped breakfast rushing back. Before we left, Brownie quietly slipped me back the envelope of cash I'd returned to him.

"Just in case there's something going on we don't know about, I'd like to keep you on retainer."

Philadelphia Long's Tavern & English Tearoom are two establishments that fill the entire first floor of a four-story brick building on Cutter Avenue. The Tavern is an English-style pub that fills the larger space while the Tearoom is cozy with lace-covered tables and an English cottage garden for outside dining. As it was a warm spring day, we opted for the garden patio. The Tearoom is a popular haven for femmes and lipsticks, so Sonny got a lot of appreciative looks as we passed through.

I ordered a three-egg omelet filled with fresh greens and Gruyere cheese, rye toast and a pot of Earl Grey. Sonny had an omelet with everything, a side of grilled veggies and an herbal tea. She seemed distracted and a bit on edge. As was my bent for conducting interviews, I waited until Sonny was ready to tell me what bothered her.

"The police want to see me."

"Do you know why?"

"They want to know where I was Sunday, and what I know about Ron Brinkman's death. The thing is, I don't know anything. I didn't even know he was dead."

"Who told you he was dead?"

"Jacky."

"When?"

"This morning. You see . . . ," Sonny blushed.

"Take your time. No rush."

Sonny poured more tea and sipped it.

"As I told you before, my marriage to Jacky wasn't all bad. In many ways, he was good to me. Anyway, around midnight Saturday, Jacky called me at the Bistro. This was after you saw him, he said. He wanted to apologize for Brinkman's harassment. Said he hadn't known, but it wouldn't happen again. We got to talking and remembering old times. Not his cheating and the breakup. Better times. It was nice, so I asked if he'd like to go to my aunt's for Easter. Said he'd like that. I picked him up at the Marriot around 10:00 or so Sunday morning and we crossed the river. We had a good time at my aunt's, and after that we . . ."

Sonny paused. Sipped more tea.

"Anyway, we were having such a good time together, we decided not to return right away. We . . . we ended up getting a motel room near the river and spent Sunday night . . . and all of Monday and Monday night over there."

"And your cell phones were off the entire time?"

"Yes. When we left the Marriot. We weren't trying to avoid anyone but didn't want to be bothered with calls. We didn't think to turn them on again until this morning. Jacky turned his on first to check for messages. That's when he learned the police wanted to get in touch. He called them and spoke with a Detective Lockhart. That's when we learned of Brinkman's death, and how I know they want to see me too. My phone's still off. I know that once I turn it on and hear my messages, I'll have to call. I'm not sure what to do."

"Where's Fry now?"

"Probably talking with Detective Lockhart. I dropped him at the Marriot just before coming to the Bistro. He said he was going to change then go see the police."

"Lockhart interviewed me yesterday about my whereabouts. One of my business cards was found in Brinkman's room. As far as I know, he's just looking for information and not accusing anyone of anything. So I suggest you turn your phone on and call him and set up an appointment. However, you might want to take a lawyer with you."

"Do I need one?"

"The police would say innocent people don't need

lawyers. My lawyer would disagree. Many innocent people seem to get arrested and end up convicted of crimes they didn't commit. I think often because they don't have a lawyer at all police interviews. Would you like me to call mine and see if she'll be there with you?"

Sonny nodded. I called Carmen and filled her in. She said that her partner, Truman Pfeiffer, was free this afternoon and could handle it.

"Carmen's partner is free and can be there. Make your call."

Sonny turned on her phone and checked messages; then called the number for Lockhart. She spoke with him for a couple minutes, turned to me and mouthed the words "three-thirty."

"Carmen, will 3:30 work for Truman?"

I nodded to Sonny. She confirmed that time with Lockhart and we both hung up.

"Truman Pfeiffer will meet you in the lobby of Police Central at 3:20. He'll have a form for you to sign and you should give him this."

I gave her $1,000 out of the stack of cash Brownie had given me as a retainer. Sonny tried to hand it back.

"Don't worry about it. It's from Brownie. He'd want you to use it. Also, part of it will come back to me through Andrews & Pfeiffer as their staff investigator. Now, anything you say to me falls under their attorney/client privilege protection."

"What happens now?"

"We finish lunch. You go take a shower and try to relax for your interview, and I'll head out to the Marriot to see what I can discover."

Nineteen

Before reaching the Marriot I got a call from Frank Taylor confirming that there was no Claude Akins or anyone of his description working on a farm or ranch in Washington County.

"I'm certain this is your shooter, Rachel. I've sent a courier down to pick up a blood sample Sheriff Walker's deputies got from the trauma center. I'm sure it will match what we got from your condo."

"Thanks, Frank. I expected as much. Any other leads?"

"No. But I was told his hand was pretty messed up. It'll be awhile before he can use it. Also, I checked on Cheswick and Thorton. They're still squirrelled away at Club Fed, and it doesn't look like they're involved. Just to be sure, the warden's checking back communications they've had and will monitor closely what they're doing now."

"Thanks. Don't really think they're behind it, but better safe than sorry."

At the Marriot I went looking for the head of security and was introduced to Frank Gallop and explained my interest in Brinkman's death.

"Can't tell you much. Our security system went schizoid late Saturday night and we couldn't get the problem ironed out until yesterday. Circuit breakers kept tripping at various locales. As a result we have very little video backup of hotel activity for the weekend. Also, being Easter Sunday, most of our housekeeping staff was off. We were only cleaning rooms where guests checked out or had specifically asked for service. The police aren't happy about our problem either, but what can you do? It is what it is."

"What can you tell me for sure about Brinkman?"

"Well, just before our cameras went berserko, this was around 11:30 Saturday night, Brinkman entered the lobby alone and went into the bar and grill. According to the barman, he ordered a double Scotch & water and met a blonde woman wearing a red cocktail dress. The barman wasn't sure if they knew each other previously or not. They had a couple of drinks that were put on Brinkman's tab and left together. No camera saw where they went.

"Around 9:00 the next morning, a working camera caught Brinkman and what appeared to be the same woman—still wearing the cocktail dress, by the way—go into the hotel restaurant for breakfast. A waitress confirmed seeing them. They were there less than an hour. Again, the cameras went blooey, so there's no telling where they went after that. Brinkman wasn't seen again until one of the maids found him dead Monday.

"There was no 'Do Not Disturb' sign on his door Monday morning, so the maid went in to freshen the room. The bed wasn't made, but she heard the shower running, so she called out an apology and said she'd be back later. When she went back about noon just before her lunch break, the shower was still going. That's where she discovered the body. That's about all I can say without getting in Dutch with the authorities."

"So Brinkman was definitely alive Sunday morning, but no one saw him again after that."

"That's about it."

"The blonde woman. Any chance she was a registered guest?"

"Doubtful. Police did a sketch based on the barman's and

waitress' description, but no one on the desk remembers anyone like her checking in or out. No other staff members recall her either."

"Think she's a hooker or just a catch-as-catch-can?"

"Wouldn't want to speculate."

"Could I speak with the barman, the waitress and the maid who found the body?"

"Police asked that they not give any interviews at this time to anyone. Sorry."

"Like you said, 'it is what it is.' Thanks for your time and help."

"Hey, you came to me directly and stated your needs. You didn't go sneaking around like some do and hassling the staff. That's respectful. Respect deserves respect. Come back anytime."

"Thanks. Here's a couple of my cards if you or a guest ever need a private service."

I called Truman Pfeiffer and filled him in on what I'd found out so he'd be ready when Sonny was questioned.

"Want me to follow up and try and find the woman?"

"Not yet. You've done enough for now. I appreciate the heads-up. Let's wait and see what the ME decides on cause of death. No need to waste time and dollars if there's no crime."

That out of the way, I drove out to Belle's Diner. I didn't know if things were completely back to normal for the girls, or not. I'd gotten a good feeling from Isabella the night I brought Maria home, but you never know. And my plan with Kerri depended a lot on normalcy. I couldn't be sure that I'd see any of the girls, but school should be letting out and I hoped to catch them walking home. If not, I'd do a drive around to see what I could see.

At Belle's, Lisa was on, and her nametag this time was Sandy. We talked briefly about my finding Maria, and I thanked her for her help. Then I ordered a chocolate shake and a basket of fries and took a booth so I could look out the window. I saw a few girls dressed in Sacred Heart uniforms, but not the ones I wanted. Maybe I missed them already.

Halfway through my fries, I saw Maria, Emily and Lauren coming out of the library across the street. They were laughing and headed for the convenience store. Emily and Lauren were in their school uniforms. Maria was wearing jeans and a sweatshirt and carrying her bookbag. Looked heavy. A few minutes later, they passed by and I ducked down in my seat. I didn't want them knowing I was checking on them. Didn't want word possibly getting back to Elena or Taylor. Maria and Emily were sharing an Almond Joy bar. Lauren was eating a Fudgsicle. Three young teens who looked like they hadn't a care in the world. That was okay with me. I finished my fries and shake.

From Belle's I went to Cramer College and drove past the house. There were three cars in the drive that I'd seen before. I parked and watched for an hour. There were some comings and goings, but—thankfully—no underaged teens. I didn't see any surveillance. Maybe Kerri hadn't assigned any yet. Then again, they probably weren't meant to be seen. Knowing Kerri, I had to assume they were there. Had to assume if any kids went in, the raid would immediately follow.

I went back to the office and did another search on Ethan Fletcher, just for something to do. Nothing came up. What if he changed his name and identity? I tried to remember what he looked like, tried to age that image 15 years and maybe 20 or 30 pounds. No, he wasn't the guy. I remembered that Fletcher was over six feet. This guy was my height. So who? Why? Who had I pissed off?

I thought about Henry Seiko who killed Karen and nearly killed Wendy. I killed him. To the best of my knowledge, the police haven't discovered if that was his real identity or not. He had assumed so many. And as no one claimed his body, he was buried in a pauper's grave at City Cemetery. Was he the reason for my attack? Think, woman. Think! Seiko was Japanese or Japanese-American. This guy obviously isn't. Where's the connection?

Damn it to hell! Who the fuck wants me dead? Frustration always leaves me hungry. It hadn't been that long since I finished that basket of fries and shake, and I felt I was starving. I head for Charlie's and a slaw and chili dog.

Twenty

The **Wednesday morning edition** of *The Daily Record* had a brief article that the body found Monday at the Marriot was that of Ronald Brinkman, a New York-based entertainment agent. Police were awaiting cause of death results from the medical examiner's office but would appreciate any calls from the general public with any relevant information.

Sonny called wondering if I'd heard anything new on Brinkman's death. She thanked me for letting Pfeiffer know that Brinkman died sometime after she and Fry were at her aunt's home. That was a relief as she and Jacky had both worried about being suspects if his death was ruled a homicide. As for her and Fry getting back together after their weekend fling, it wasn't going to happen.

"Been there. Done that. Best that'll happen is we reconcile a lasting friendship."

I told her I hadn't heard anything new, but that I or Pfeiffer would keep her updated.

Kerri called at 2:15 to update me on Saturday's planned raid.

"My guys downloaded a bunch of photos from that website you gave me. We also found a second site with some of the same pictures and are still checking other sites as well.. Based on those and the other stuff you gave me, I've secured warrants to search the whole house, out-buildings and vehicles, gather any and all photographs and cameras as well as video recordings and video making devices including computers and cell phones—basically, anything I want—as well as any drugs we find. We can also photograph and take evidence of any place that corresponds to where the online videos were made. I also have arrest warrants for specific individuals and several John and Jane Doe warrants.

"I can go in at any time I choose. I'll try to hold off until Saturday, but I have to say I already have the house under surveillance. If any underaged children go in, I'll raid the place immediately. I hope you understand that."

So I was right about surveillance. "Perfectly. I wouldn't expect otherwise. How many know this is happening?"

"Just you, me, the judge who signed my warrants, and my team leaders who gathered the evidence. No one in my chain or PR has been alerted, or will be, until this goes down. I'm keeping it on the QT to prevent leaks. If the word gets out to anyone, I won't wait. I'll have to go in. Have you told anyone?"

"Only Wendy to reassure her that I'm doing something to end this situation. However, . . ."

"However, what?"

"I'd like to give two reporters I know a heads-up of the raid."

"Why? I thought you wanted anonymity."

"I do. I trust these two not to involve me in any way in exchange for a hot tip. That's part of my reasoning. At the same time, I want to see the arrests of the adults make headlines which, hopefully, will encourage plea deals and help keep child victims out of any court proceedings. Thirdly, it'd be best if such a tip couldn't be traced back to you or anyone in your section."

"Damn straight on that. So, who've you got in mind to risk your reputation and my pension?"

"Tanya Waverly, news anchor at Channel 3, and Andy Walther at *The Daily Record*."

"That's it?"

"That's it."

Kerri was quiet for several minutes.

"Okay. I know them. They're fair-minded and competent. Hope I don't regret this. Tell you what, if things go down the way we plan Saturday, they get a 30-minute jump on their competitors. That's the best I can do. I won't act pleased to see them, but I'll issue a short statement and answer two questions at the scene exclusively to them. I'll give you a five-minute warning that we're going in. So have them close by but don't give them the address until I give you the word. I don't want to know any arrangements you make with them. This conversation never happened."

"Understood."

I was feeling good about the pending raid and planning what to say to Tanya and Andy when my phone rang. I didn't recognize the number.

"This is Rachel Cord. How may I help you."

"Hi, Ms. Cord. It's Maria."

"Maria. I'm surprised to hear from you. Is everything all right?"

"Yes. I just wanted to thank you again for taking me home and protecting my friends."

"You're welcome, but I was just doing my job."

"Well, thank you. You were right about how to handle Elena. She's been super nice. Taylor too. I think they're still afraid I'm going to rat on them."

Not half as afraid as they're going to be. "That's good to hear. So, you're not permanently grounded?"

"No, *Señora* Isabella has been very kind. I can even go to the library alone. But she asks me to let her know where I go. She even gave me a cell phone so I can stay in touch. I'm at the library now."

"Wow, a cell phone. Sounds great. Does that mean you gals are doing the usual Saturday movie and mall crawl?"

"That's the plan, but it still bothers me. I know Elena and Taylor are going to do their thing. I wish they'd stop, but I know they won't. I'm really sorry for Brittany though. That she's going with them now. They're just using her. They don't care about her at all."

"Maybe you can talk her into staying with you and the others."

"I doubt it. She's wants to be like them too much. Anyway, Emily, Lauren and I are more interested in the Harry Potter meeting Sunday here at the library. It got postponed a week because of Easter. We can't wait for the last book to come out this summer. We're all trying to figure out how Harry will defeat Voldemort."

"That sounds like fun. Glad things are back to normal for you."

"Me too. Bye"

Somehow, I didn't think normal would be happening for a long time come Saturday.

There was nothing new on the guy trying to kill me. No news is not necessarily good news.

Twenty-One

With nothing really to do at the office, I stayed home Thursday and tried a couple of cosmetic products to remove the last of the gunpowder stippling my face. Worked out better than expected. I could go back to my normal makeup routine.

Doris called to say that the morning mail included full payment from Valerie Danzigar with a $1,500 bonus and two personal letters for a job well done from her and her lawyers. Also, one of the pending accounts paid their bill and — surprise of surprises — the Rizelli brothers sent a check for half of what they owed with a promise to pay the rest within 45 days.

On that high note, I enjoyed a workout on the personal gym equipment Wendy installed in what had been Karen's former studio followed by a luxuriously long hot shower.

After my shower, I called Andy Walther and Tanya Waverly about the pending raid that was going down Saturday.

"I can't explain right now, but trust me, this is a story you'll want. If you're interested, we can meet tomorrow at Phil's English Tavern. I can give you details then about when and where to be Saturday morning."

Near noon, Frank Taylor called saying he had a good lead narrowing the ID of our shooter from 40 percent of the male population down to a handful of possibilities.

"How about meeting me at Charlie's and I'll tell you all about it."

Not wanting to spoil Frank's penchant for sharing good news over a good hot dog—or any news for that matter—we agreed to meet in an hour.

I left our condo parking lot going north on River Drive and stopping at the light at Cutter Avenue. Made the left onto Cutter and headed for my lunch meeting with Frank at Charlie's. I heard a squeal of tires and glanced in my rearview mirror. A dusty and faded white Ford pickup that had been behind me was accelerating quickly and passing in the left lane. As it came alongside, I glimpsed the twin barrels of a shotgun sticking out the window. I hit the brakes hard and the double blast went across the front of my car. For the second time in less than a week I saw the flash and fire of a gun going off in my face.

I came to a full stop shoving the gears into park. The Ford pulled in front of me and screeched to a stop. I drew my gun as I got out of the car and fired one shot at the Ford's cab just behind where the driver's head should be. The Ford suddenly pulled away. Before I could get off a second shot, a car's horn behind me made me jump. I turned holding my hands up and out to the side.

What? Can't you see I'm shooting here? The horn-blasting driver's eyes went wide as she disappeared from view. I looked to the curb and saw that instead of my head, the shotgun blast had taken out the front window of Phil's Tearoom.

Damn. I re-holstered my gun, called 911, and went to see if anyone inside were hurt. Broken glass was strewn everywhere but I was relieved to see that no one had been standing in the entry area. As I spoke with the 911 dispatcher, Elspeth Glencannon, the tearoom manager, came around the corner.

"Rachel, what happened?" As always, Elspeth's Highland burr gave me a warm feeling even if it wasn't appropriate to the moment.

"Anyone hurt?"

"Don't think so; nearly everyone's on the patio. Let me check."

Dying sirens and brake sounds made it hard to hear the dispatcher.

"There don't seem to be any injuries, we're double checking now. What? A 'crazy woman with a gun?' I think that's supposed to be me."

Elspeth came back. "No one's hurt."

I nodded. "Yes, operator, I understand. No, there are no injuries. Yes, I'm coming outside now. Please inform the officers the only thing in my hands is the phone I'm speaking to you with. Okay, no phone either. Elspeth, stay inside."

I left the phone on and put it in my pocket, opened the door and stuck my hands out first, my fingers widely splayed.

"I'm coming out. No gun. Don't shoot."

"That's her! That's her! She threatened me with a gun!"

The horn-blasting driver was standing behind a police car pointing at me.

"Lie on the ground! Hands away from your body!"

Looking at the dirty sidewalk, I regretted choosing to wear my alpaca trousers and jacket. Hope the cleaners can get any stains out. I felt a knee on my back and a hand roughly grabbed my right wrist and pulled it behind me. I was quickly handcuffed.

"My gun is holstered behind my back and my ID and permits are in the left jacket pocket. The phone in my right pocket is still connected to the 911 dispatcher."

As the officer searched me and led me to his car, I gave a

brief summary of what occurred adding, "and I did not point my gun at or threaten that woman." A few minutes later the door on the other side of the car opened and Frank Taylor climbed in.

"Thought we were meeting at Charlie's?"

"Me, too. But as you see, I got delayed."

"You do realize you loused up my lunch routine again, don't you?"

"Sorry for that. I'm ready to go anytime you are, if you can get me released."

"So what happened?"

Frank took notes as I gave a detailed statement reiterating emphatically that I hadn't threatened Ms. Horn-blaster or anyone else.

"Get a license number from the truck?"

"No. Horn-blaster spooked me before I got it all. It was a specialty plate I'll say that. Part of an American flag, I think: white stars on blue, some wavy red and white bars. Maybe a figure or badge. Black letters and numbers. First two could be D-A or D-4 or 0-A or 0-4; something like that anyway. Could even be out-of-state, for all I know. There are just too many plates to know anymore."

"Back in a minute."

Seemed like forever before the car door opened and the officer who cuffed me helped me out and removed the handcuffs. He did not, however, give me back my gun.

Frank walked over. "I'm riding with you. We have three witness statements so far that pretty much match your version, so you're not under arrest yet. There's an BOLO out for the Ford pickup, but no one else caught the plate either. Some of the heavier traveled streets are video monitored, so we could get lucky on the plate yet. Marty's going to supervise here while Forensics locates all of the buckshot and gets tire residue or other evidence from the street. Some uniforms are also checking neighboring businesses to see if any security cams caught any of the action. Marty'll pick me up later at Charlie's."

"What about my gun?"

"That depends on what the DA decides to do. Your horn-blower signed a complaint, and you *did* fire your gun on a public street."

"That was self defense. Great. There's a guy out there trying to kill me and you confiscate my gun."

"I'm sure you'll think of something."

"So what's the hot lead on who he is?"

"I was going to tell you that over lunch, remember? Let's go."

While Frank waited on our order at Charlie's — my treat — I made several short calls: first to Wendy and then Doris and Mary to let them know I was all right and not to take any calls from any inquiring media jackals wanting a story; then a call to my lawyer filling her in on what happened. Carmen said she'd follow up on it and try to get my gun released as soon as possible. Not trusting the system to work as quickly, or as efficiently, as I thought it should, I called my gun dealer to see if he had a replacement in stock. He did and I could get it whenever I wanted. I said I'd be by in an hour or so.

Finally, to try and head off any misleading media reports, I called Andy Walther and Tanya Waverly and off-the-record confirmed that I was the one targeted by the shooting on Cutter Avenue, and that Phil's Tearoom getting hit was a complete accident and not some new form of gay bashing. I asked that they try and get the story as little play as possible and said we were still meeting the next day.

"And, no, this has nothing to do with the hot tip I've got for you."

Hmmm. Gay bashing. I hadn't thought of that as a possible motive for killing me. I've never hidden — except when I was

141

in the Army—what I am, but was I that well-known to be considered a target for the cause? Far fetched, but people had been killed for less.

Frank returned with our order. We didn't get around to talking until he'd finished his first Chicago dog and I was halfway through my messy slaw and chili dog.

"Glad to see that being shot at hasn't spoiled your appetite."

"I'm more angry than scared right now, and angry makes me hungry." Anger. Frustration. Being Horny. Okay, lots of things make me hungry.

"I can relate to that, but I wish you'd be more scared and consider leaving town. We're narrowing in on this guy and we'll catch him."

"I'm sure you are and that you will, but I've still got business to finish first." I took another bite before continuing. "There's a song I heard the other day, *The Bad Bitch Blues*. It had a line something like 'you don't mess with a woman who's got the bad bitch blues.' That's me right now. I'm mad and I'm angry. 'Bad Bitch' angry. This guy has no idea who he's messing with."

"Rachel, it's our job to catch this guy. Don't go looking for him. I'd hate to see you go to prison if he ends up dead."

"I know, and I hope you catch him soon. I just want to be ready if he comes looking for me again."

We finished our hot dogs in silence.

"Rachel, what do you know about familial DNA searching?"

"Nothing. Why?"

"It's fairly new and controversial. I don't understand it exactly, but basically it's getting a near enough DNA match to someone already in the system, that the person you're looking for must be a close relative; like brothers and sisters or fathers and sons. That sort of thing. It helped catch that BTK killer over in Kansas and some guy in the UK before that."

"And this helps us how?"

"I ran some DNA test results through our system this morning. A near match came back almost instantly."

"DNA results? I thought you weren't expecting any results for weeks at best?"

"Apparently Wendy had a private lab run a sample and gave us the results this morning. Though they aren't official, I thought why not? Couldn't hurt and might give us a lead. I was surprised at the hit that came back."

"Wendy gave you results of a DNA test?"

"Actually, she had the lab deliver them to me direct. As I said, they aren't official—poor chain of evidence—and probably wouldn't hold up in court. But considering who they're linked to, I think we'll get the same result eventually from our own samples. Didn't she tell you about it?"

"No, she didn't. I remember her being upset when I said it could be weeks or even months before you got official results. And I remember a bloodstain still on the doorjamb Saturday night, and her saying she'd take care of it. I had no idea she'd use it to get a DNA test done. That sneaky . . . adorable— Okay, tell me. Whose name popped out?"

"Alan Wilson."

"The College Park Strangler?"

"One and the same. And you caught him."

"I hadn't gotten around to thinking about him. Wasn't he finally executed?"

"No, he's still on Death Row. The state hasn't executed anyone for nearly two years. Declared a moratorium shortly before his execution date. There's talk of lifting it this summer. Far as I know, Wilson's near the top of the list."

"And some close relative would like to see me dead before that happens. Is that it?"

"That's as good a hypothesis as any. Narrows the field of

suspects one hell of a lot."

"I guess it does. Any idea which relative?"

"Not yet, but we're checking. Like I said, we're going to get this guy. So, please, lie low and stay safe."

"Yeah, right." Like that's going to happen.

When **I arrived at A to Z** Weaponry, the parking lot was nearly full, but the main showroom had fewer than a dozen customers. Most of the customers were looking at shotguns, while three in cammies were discussing what looked to me to be a Bushmaster AR-15 variant with a salesman. There were several different-sized magazines on the counter. Although the showroom was quiet, floor vibration told me the basement gun range was active.

I saw the storeowner, Morrie David, standing behind a counter helping a customer fill out paperwork. He saw me and pointed toward the revolver display where I met him a few minutes later.

"Hey, Morrie, how's business?"

"Brisk with spring hunting opening."

"Surely those Bushmaster lookers aren't planning on using that on snow geese and wild turkeys?"

"Think they're going to some western state that has a spring season on deer or elk."

Having trained and qualified with the M16A2 military version, I've never quite understood why so-called sportsmen and hunters have an affection—or need—for such a military-styled assault weapon to kill Bambi or Bullwinkle. Maybe it's a testosterone-driven desire to "play Army" for grown-ups. I don't know. Seems like massive overkill to me.

"Anyway, that's not why you're here." Morrie reached under the counter and brought up a box with my replacement Smith & Wesson 340PD. "One of my salespeople heard a radio report of a shooting incident down on Cutter Avenue. Your

144

name was mentioned. What happened? The police confiscate the last one of these I sold you?"

"Something like that."

"As you're here, I take it you weren't arrested. Guess I can sell this to you. Need ammo or anything?"

"No. I've got two speedloaders in the car waiting to be used."

"So, when you gonna switch to a real gun?"

I smiled. There are those who prefer the semi-automatics, the Glocks, Berettas and such, with their larger capacity firepower. I'll admit there's much to be said in favor of returning a lot of lead in a firefight. Pull the trigger enough times, after all, and you're bound to hit something. But I prefer my five-shot S&W despite reports of inaccuracy. That's a problem I've not experienced when I've needed to use it. I like it's small and lightweight scandium alloy frame that fits my hand; that it's hammerless with a short barrel that doesn't get caught on anything no matter where I carry it; best of all, it uses full load, 158-grain .357 Magnum rounds. Besides, I already had the holster for it.

"Think I'll stick with what I know."

"Suit yourself. Cash or credit?"

"Credit. Wait a minute. You sell soft body armor too, don't you?"

"We carry some or we can special order for you. What are you looking for?"

Twenty-Two

I **walked out of the Aeropostle store** at the crowded mall and looked around. I didn't see any of the girls. I turned and headed for the food court not sure why I was looking for them. Why was I even in the store? How did I get here? Out of the corner of my eye, I glimpsed a man in a hoodie with a heavily bandaged right hand walking the other way. I couldn't see his face but turned to follow.

As much as I hurried to catch up to him, he stayed ahead of me. He seemed to flow through the crowd, while I was continually being blocked. He went up the escalator to the second level and wandered around, in and out of various stores, not buying anything. He didn't look back at me. I needed to get a good look at him. See if he was the one trying to kill me. I reached behind my back to be sure my gun was there. It wasn't. And I realized I wasn't wearing my body armor either, which made no sense. I had just bought it and didn't plan to go anywhere without it. I knew I shouldn't continue to pursue him, but I had to know who he was.

He went down a side corridor. Then another. The crowds were thinning. Disappearing until we were alone. The mall lights dimmed except for the hallway ahead. He became a dark sillouette leading me. He rounded a corner. I raced to catch up. He had entered an elevator. As the door closed, he looked up. I stared into the grinning face of Alan Wilson.

"Rachel. Rachel. Wake up. You're dreaming."

Wendy was shaking me. Morning sunlight, glimmering around the drapes to our bedroom balcony, gave the room a soft glow. I was breathing heavily.

"Are you all right?"

I nodded. "Yes, I think so. I was having a nightmare. Give me a moment."

My body felt clammy and I was suddenly chilled. I could still see Wilson's smiling face. Wendy held me in her arms. We lay like that for quite some time. I had had trouble falling asleep the night before obsessing over Wilson and whichever of his relatives was after me. His presence continued to smother me. Wendy kissed me softly. I relished her warmth. We made love, my clinging desperately to her to escape the horror in my head. We showered together and had breakfast. Wendy left for work unsure if she should leave me alone.

"I'm fine. Go. I'm just going to stay here and go over the plans for the raid.

I jumped when my phone rang midmorning. I hoped it was Frank calling that he'd finally IDed my shooter. Even cuddling with Wendy hadn't cured my nervousness.

I hadn't been a PI long back in '98, when the father of one of the five women raped and murdered in College Park hired me to help find the killer. Without much information to go on, I played bait several nights at the park. Not the smartest move, but the only plan I had at the time. It also paid out.

Just as I was ready to give up, a uniformed cop offered to escort me from the park. There were things that made me think he was bogus, and he was leading me the wrong way. I managed to take him down and call for the real police. The phony was Alan Wilson. Evidence was later found to connect him to all five murders.

He lawyered up and never spoke with the police. Nor did he testify at his trial. I remembered his constant stare and smile while I was on the stand. I'd no doubt then, or now, as to what he wanted to do to me. And one of his relatives was trying to make that happen. Yes, I definitely hoped it was Frank calling with good news.

"Ms. Cord, it's Detective Lockhart. As I said when we last met, I'd let you know when I had information I could share on Ronald Brinkman's death."

"Ouch. Is that a subtle slap, detective, for my not calling when I saw Sonny Tristan Tuesday morning?"

"I thought about it, but no. Had you called right away you would have interrupted my interview with Jacky Fry, and as it was, I probably wouldn't have seen Ms. Tristan any sooner Tuesday than I did. I suppose I *should* thank you for Ms. Tristan having her lawyer present though."

"Ouch, again."

Lockhart laughed. "Anyway, I'm just keeping my promises. We got the ME report. Ronald Brinkman died of a heart attack while taking a shower Sunday afternoon. Yes, you were right in suspecting there were suspicious aspects about his death. Specifically, there were several bruises to his face and head that could have been caused by blunt force trauma."

"But it wasn't?"

"No. The ME report and Forensics' evidence show that the bruises occurred during Mr. Brinkman's heart attack by his first striking his face on the shower faucet; then when he stumbled from the shower, he fell and struck his forehead on the toilet seat; and finally, he fell back into the shower and struck the back of his head on the shower wall. At least that's the most logical scenario based upon available data. Much of the evidence was obliterated by the continuously running shower until he was found Monday."

"What about the blonde in the red dress he was with?"

"Ah, so you did do some homework. We spoke with her and confirmed that she left the hotel at 11:45 a.m. by taxi and wasn't there when he died. Nor were your client or Mr. Fry who were across the river at the probable time of death."

"So there was no crime?"

"That's correct. I informed Truman Pfeiffer of this before calling you."

"Thank you for letting me know."

"Not a problem. As I said, just keeping my promises. Have a nice day."

"You too."

I called Sonny to see if she'd heard the news. She'd just spoken to Pfeiffer and was relieved and thankful. Said she was going to call Fry and let him know.

Andy Walther, Tanya Waverly and I met over ploughman's lunches and beer at Phil's Tavern to discuss our meet-up in the morning. I personally prefer the Tearoom for ambiance, but being styled as an English pub, the Tavern has several alcoves that work well for semi-private discussions.

"The Sex Crime Division is going to conduct a major raid tomorrow between 11:00 a.m. and 1:00 p.m. near Cramer College. Most likely closer to noon."

Andy and Tanya exchanged glances and both said they hadn't gotten any heads-up from their police contacts.

"This involves Internet child pornography. Because children may be present when the raid goes down, the division chief, Lt. Kerri Trujillo, has kept it on a strict need to know to prevent leaks and causing a media frenzy. That meant only her people and didn't include higher ups or the department PR."

Andy asked the obvious. "How do you know and why are we especially privileged?"

"Off the record, I gave Lt. Trujillo the original tip and much of the back-up evidence that got her the search and arrest warrants. I came across it as a tangent to a runaway case I was working. As for you two, I like you guys and we trade info and favors occasionally. I also trust you. Lt. Trujillo's reasoning is along similar lines as mine. She wants to see the perps' arrests made public as much as I do. However, she can't risk being the tipster or appear to know that you were alerted. She is prepared, though, to make a short off-the-cuff statement and answer a couple of questions to whatever press that just happen to show up. That means you two. You should get about a 30-minute jump on your competitors."

"Sounds good to me. How do we handle the timing?" Tanya asked.

"We meet at the north parking lot of College Park before 11:00 and wait. We'll be less than two minutes from the house being raided; I've already traced the shortest route. Trujillo will call me a few minutes before they go in so that you have time to arrive and photo her people entering. So have your photographer or cameraman ready to shoot as you roll up."

"Not that I expect anyone to ask," Andy put in, "but what should we use as an excuse for being at the scene?"

"Right after calling me, Trujillo will notify the police dispatcher over official police radio that she's about to serve warrants on a particular address involved in Internet child pornography. You could say you had an anonymous tip that something was going to happen near the college, so you were already in the area and monitoring police frequencies when the word went out. You journalists do it all the time."

Tanya ordered another round of beer. "Okay, we're protected by the First Amendment, and Trujillo's covered her ass by using you. What do *you* want in exchange?"

"Total anonymity. Absolutely no mention of me, or any PI, being the source of information. It could jeopardize a sensitive resolution to the case I just finished."

"That's it?"

"That's it."

"Okay. I'll see you by 10:45 tomorrow at College Park. Let me know if we need to be there sooner or if there are any last minute changes. Thanks for the tip. I hate to eat and run, but I've an interview to do before the Evening Report." Tanya took out her wallet as she got up.

I stopped her. "Lunch is on me."

Tanya nodded but put $5 on the table toward the tip. Andy sat back and finished his beer.

"Seems like you've got this pretty well under control. Hope it plays out the way you want."

"Me too. Know who your photographer will be?"

"Clyde Normand. He's the best we've got; he already knows you; and he can keep a secret beyond the grave. Another round?"

"Not for me, but I'll buy you another. Two's my limit when I'm driving. Actually, I should have stopped at one as I'm also carrying."

"Right. I'm surprised the cops didn't confiscate your gun yesterday."

"They did. This is a new one."

"Any news on the guy who's targeting you?"

"Police are checking some leads but nothing solid."

Our waiter brought Andy's beer and I paid the check.

"I haven't asked in a while, but have you thought about the book I suggested we write?"

"Not at all."

I had to smile. The book, *Confessions of Madame Gumshoe by Rachel Cord as told to Andy Walther,* had become a running joke between us the past three years. If written, it would delve deeply into what actually happened at Calvin Tierney's property: my rape, my killing of Tierney and Gwen Archer. A story that I had only fully revealed to my rape survivor group and very few others. Had I healed enough to share it with Andy, with others? That the suggestion of writing my story — putting my life and darkest moments out to the world — could make me smile, may mean I'd finally taken complete control of the incident. That it no longer held any power over me.

"Tell you what. This isn't for general knowledge yet, but I'm going to Florida next month to finally get rid of this albatross of mine. I'll be recovering for several weeks before going back to work fulltime. So I'll give doing a book some serious thought. If I decide yes, we could work on it then."

"Whenever you're ready, just let me know."

Frank called saying he'd IDed the guy trying to kill me, though they still hadn't located him.

"We're 98 percent sure that he's Paul Harvey Beauxdreaux. It's pronounced Boo-DROW, but spelled B-e-a-u-x-d-r-e-a-u-x. He's Alan Wilson's first cousin. Their mothers are sisters. He's a volunteer firefighter in Mount Ararat, Kentucky, pop less than 8,000. That's somewhere near Louisville, I'm told. He owns a white Ford 150 with license plate 'DAWG 1' that matches closely the plate you described. He's supposedly on vacation on a hunting trip."

"Yeah, me."

"Right. He and Wilson were as close as kids can get growing up back there and has visited Wilson several times in prison the past few years. The guy has a clean record and is well liked in his community. He's married, two kids, regular churchgoer.

"Sheriff there has his doubts this is our guy. However, the fire department keeps DNA records of their personnel in case anyone gets lost in a fire, or is otherwise unidentifiable, and can't be positively IDed. It's a small town, but they lost three firefighters in a severe wildfire some years back. Apparently, they had to resort to dental and DNA for the IDs. Now they keep that info in their system. The Sheriff is faxing us a copy of Beauxdreaux's DNA file to compare with our data as well as a recent photograph of him.

"Also, the warden at State Prison is sending us a photo of

the guy who's been visiting Wilson recently. He was last there two weeks ago. That'll cinch our last two percent of doubt as to ID and why he's targeting you. Now we just need to find him."

"So where is this guy?"

"That's hard to say. We have a multi-state alert out for his arrest and for information that could lead to that arrest. Just a matter of time before he or his truck are spotted."

"Meanwhile, I keep looking over my shoulder."

"'Fraid so. I'll get back to you when I know more."

I updated Wendy on what was happening that evening. We were both glad that the raid was finally happening and on edge about where my assassin was. It was a numb night of mindless TV and troubled sleep as every odd sound kept awakening us.

Twenty-Three

The raid went exactly as planned. Andy and Clyde, and Tanya with a two-man crew, showed up at the parking lot at 10:45. We shared donuts and coffee that I brought while we waited. I was still yawning from my sleepless night.

Kerri called at 11:40. "Girls arriving. We go in six minutes."

I led our small convoy and, as I had promised, we were there in less than two minutes. I pulled over short of the site, but Andy and Tanya closed in. I saw Clyde and Tanya's cameraman jump out before their vehicles barely stopped. I turned off and went to Cramer College and climbed their clock tower that's open to the public. From there I could get a good view of what was happening with binoculars.

Kerri appeared agitated and waved the photographers away as they began shooting pictures. Then she threw up her hands in despair, and she and her team entered the house two minutes early, by my watch. I saw Tanya's other crewmember setting up a portable dish antenna and checking instruments at the van. Tanya and her cameraman, and Andy and Clyde waited at the edge of the property.

At 12:01, Kerri came out on the porch. She seemed to be arguing with someone on her cell phone. She held a hand up as if to keep cameras and reporters back. She put her phone away and approached the reporters at the curb. My phone rang. It was Wendy.

"Channel 3 has a live broadcast of that sex raid on their Noon Report. Are you there?"

"I'm up in Cramer College's clock tower, but I can see what's happening. What's Kerri saying?"

"Something about not knowing how the reporters got there so quickly, but that the City Sex Crimes Division are serving search and arrest warrants on a house suspected of making Internet child pornography photos and videos."

"Videos?"

"Yes, she said, 'videos.' She now says there are five juvenile victims in the house, and she wants to remove them immediately. She's asking the reporters not to film the children leaving. She says she'll answer some quick questions after the children leave."

Five juveniles? Were Emily and Lauren somehow convinced to come along this time? And videos. I hadn't discovered those online. Only photos. I kept watching as Wendy continued explaining what was happening on the TV.

"Tanya Waverly is now on camera away from the front of the house. She's describing what she sees. Apparently a police van with darkened windows has pulled up and stopped out of camera range. She says that police officers are holding up blankets or sheets to screen victims from view. The children are being escorted as a group to the van. The van is leaving. The camera has swung around and is showing the back of the van as it goes down the street.

"The camera has swung back and is now on Kerri. A male voice—I guess that's Andy Walther—is asking how they found out about the crimes. Kerri's saying that through an anonymous tip, someone recognized a girl at a porn website who the tipster knew was only 13 and not the 18 the website claimed. The tipster also claimed to know where the photos and videos were filmed. Further investigation by the Sex Crimes Division provided enough evidence for the warrants.

The raid was made to prevent any further abuse of the victims.

"Waverly's asking how many adults have been arrested. Kerri's saying that 14 adults are in custody, but that it's not known at this time if all are involved, or if more arrests will be made. She said that they would be transporting the adults in a few minutes to Police Central, where they would be questioned further. Kerri's turned and gone back into the building. The camera is again on Waverly saying that she would have more detail of this ongoing incident on tonight's Evening Report at 6:00 and on the Late Night Report. That's the end. The studio anchor is now giving the rest of the news."

"Thanks, Wendy. I'll hang out here a bit and watch the cleanup. If you don't mind staying in, I'd like to see both of Tanya's reports tonight."

"That's okay with me. That way I won't be forced to wear that protective vest you bought."

"I thought they're light and comfortable all things considered."

"They are. Much more so and more concealable than I would have thought. I guess I don't like needing one more than anything else. Anyway, should we cook or order in to celebrate?"

"Order in. Something ethnic so we know Beauxdreaux won't be the delivery guy."

"That's not funny."

I **watched as those arrested** were brought out and put in police vehicles. Most had jackets or something hiding their faces. I was surprised that three of them appeared to be women. About the time other media began arriving, as well as Stephanie Zimmer from police PR, most of the prisoners were gone. The other four local TV stations managed to catch footage of the last three being transported. One of them was the guy with the white SUV who'd been picking up Elena and Taylor. Zimmer made a statement and took questions but Kerri did not reappear. Andy and Tanya left while others were still asking questions. My phone rang. It was Andy.

"Just wanted to say thanks for the tip. Tanya scooped me with her live report, but I'll have something in our online edition this afternoon, and this'll be front-page tomorrow. Next lunch is my tab."

Twenty-Four

As I left the clock tower to head home, my phone rang again. I didn't recognize the number and the screen only said, "Private Caller."

"This is Rachel Cord. How may I help you?"

"Ms. Cord, this is Melanie Upchurch. Brittany's mother. We've only spoken on the phone, but you interviewed Brittany when Maria Salvador went missing."

"Yes, Mrs. Upchurch, I remember. What can I do for you?"

"I . . . I've just had a call from the police. My daughter's in jail. They want me to come in as soon as possible."

"In jail? That's terrible. Did they say why she was arrested?"

"Not specifically. Only that they need to see me and would explain when I got there. I tried calling Brit but her phone is off. I . . . I'm not sure what to do. My husband's in Chicago on business. He won't be back until Wednesday. I know that you work with the police on juvenile issues, and . . . I guess I'm looking for some advice."

"You said, 'in jail.' Are you sure? Where do they want you to come?"

"Police Central. Isn't that the same thing?"

"Not quite. The City-County Jail is adjacent. That's where suspects are held after being charged and booked for a crime.

159

If Brittany hasn't been charged with anything yet, and as she's underage, the police may need you or a legal representative present in order to question her. Did the police say to which division to report?"

"No. Only that I should go to reception in the main lobby, give my name and ask for Officer Dylan or Lt. Trujillo."

"Lt. Trujillo is in charge of the Sex Crimes Division."

"Oh my God! Sex Crimes? Was my daughter raped?"

"I don't know. If she were, the police would more likely want to see you at an area hospital. Did they give you any information at all?"

"No, nothing. My poor baby."

"Try to be calm, Mrs. Upchurch. If the police gave you no reason as to why they have her in custody, don't assume the worst. It's probable she's okay. Do you know where Brittany was today?"

"She was supposed to be with her friends at the mall."

"Have you spoken with the other parents?"

"Only Rob and Penny Kennedy, Lauren's parents. Rob dropped the girls off this morning and is supposed to pick them up at 5:00. I couldn't reach the Carreras or Gatwicks. The Posterns weren't unavailable either, but Emily was staying the weekend with Maria at the Carreras."

"I see. Did you say anything to the Kennedys about the police?"

"No! That is, I said I tried to reach Brittany, but her cell phone is off, and wondered if Rob or Penny had heard anything from Lauren?"

"Had they?"

"No. But they said they'd call Lauren to see if everything was okay. Sometimes Brit forgets to turn her phone back on when she leaves the theater. I'm waiting for Penny to call me back. Just a minute, I have another call coming in. That may be Penny now."

I waited.

"Ms. Cord? Penny says that Lauren, Emily and Maria are together, but that Brit, Elena and Taylor are somewhere else at the mall. Lauren's supposed to have Brit call me as soon as they get back together."

"Except you know that the police have Brittany. I suggest you go see Lt. Trujillo right away and find out what's happening."

"Should I get a lawyer?"

"I honestly can't say without knowing what the police want. Do you have one?"

"Only for family things like wills and trusts; he doesn't handle anything like this. Would you know someone?"

"I could recommend two firms that handle juvenile cases, but that might be premature. If your lawyer is available, and as you know him already, he could probably handle anything the police need today. Brittany is only 13. I'm sure the police would like to release her to you as soon as possible. They don't like putting youngsters in the system if they can send them home."

"So maybe I won't need a lawyer yet?"

"One can't be absolutely sure of anything involving the police and criminal activity; but unless a severe crime was committed, that's been my experience."

"I don't wish to impose, but could you be there with me? I'd pay for your time."

"That's not necessary. You realize I can't give you legal advice. I'm not a lawyer."

"I understand that. As a friend of the family, then? Please, Rachel?"

I felt awkward about it, but I met Melanie Upchurch at Police Central 30 minutes later, and we were escorted to the Sex Crimes Division. Brittany was alone at a table in an interview room. She rushed to her mother when we entered.

She'd been crying and her mascara was badly smeared.

"Mom! Mom. I'm so glad you're here. It was horrible."

Melanie was nearly as distraught as her daughter as she hugged her. I could see her eyes welling with tears.

"Are you all right? Were you assaulted? Were you —?"

"No! No. Nothing like that. But they handcuffed us and everything. Take me home, mom. Please take me home."

"It'll be all right, Brit. It'll be all right. We'll go home as soon as we can."

Moments later, Kerri entered the room carrying a folder and a laptop computer.

"Mrs. Upchurch, I'm Lt. Trujillo. I'm the chief of this division. Thank you for coming down so directly."

"Why was my daughter arrested?"

"We'll get to that in just a minute. Please have a seat. Rachel, I'm surprised to see you here."

"No more surprised than I am. I advised Mrs. Upchurch that a lawyer might be more appropriate, but she asked me to come for moral support — not as a legal advisor."

I shrugged and Kerri rolled her eyes.

"Okay. Mrs. Upchurch, with your permission, I need to ask Brittany some questions before releasing her into your custody. Before I do that, however, I'd like to speak with you privately. Rachel, would you please take Brittany to the break room for a soda or something?"

"Lieutenant, I'd feel more comfortable if Ms. Cord stayed here, if you don't mind."

"Okay." Kerri stepped out the door. "Officer Dylan, would you take Brittany to the break room and get her a snack, please?"

"Mom?"

"Go with the officer, Brit."

Kerri closed the door. "Mrs. Upchurch, let me start by

saying that your daughter is physically all right and has not been charged with any crime. However, she was picked up at a house we raided this morning that's involved in Internet pornography."

"Pornography? There's no way Brittany could be involved with that. What do you mean picked up? What house? She was supposed to be at the mall with her girlfriends."

"The house is near Cramer College, Mrs. Upchurch. That's where we found your daughter and her friends this morning."

"That's impossible. I know they're at the mall."

"Not all of them, Mrs. Upchurch. Brittany and two others were at the house we raided. They had just arrived before we went in. I'm trying to determine the extent of Brittany's involvement with the pornography filmed there."

"Involvement? No way is she involved with pornography."

"I'm afraid that's not true."

Kerri opened the folder and passed Melanie a close-up photo of Brittany's face.

"This photo of your daughter is one frame from a video that we downloaded from a pornography website."

In the photo it looked to me that Brittany was hesitant and perhaps a little scared.

"Because of Brittany's age, I think she and the other girls are victims of a crime. I don't know how aware you are of child pornography on the Internet, but it is rampant to say the least."

"Are you saying that this is part of a pornographic video?"

"Yes, I am."

"Impossible."

"Mrs. Upchurch, I'm prepared to show you the whole video if you insist. I'm quite certain you won't like it." Kerri pointed to the laptop.

Melanie began shaking in disbelief. I reached over and

held her hand.

"You're saying that this is on the Internet?"

"Until a couple of hours ago, yes. We downloaded it. While we conducted a raid on where your daughter was found, the DA's office was informing the Internet Server Provider that hosts this particular website of the actual ages of some of the participants in several of the videos and photographs and requesting that the ISP immediately take down the site. Hopefully, they have complied by now."

"How did this happen?"

"That's what I'd like to ask your daughter."

Melanie took several deep breaths. "I don't want to see the video. Can you give me the gist of it?"

"From what I've seen, I don't think Brittany knew she was being videotaped, nor do I think she was experienced at what she is seen doing. This may have been her first time, I can't honestly say, but the video shows her performing oral sex on an adult male."

Tears began streaming down Melanie's face. Kerri passed her a box of tissues.

"Why would she do this? This isn't like her at all. She's so . . . I don't understand."

"I don't know, Mrs. Upchurch. I'm sorry. That's why I need to speak to Brittany. If you want a lawyer to advise you or wait for your husband to arrive, that's quite all right."

"My husband's away on business. I need to think."

"Take your time."

"Before you ask your questions, may I speak privately with my daughter?"

"Yes, certainly. Would you like a lawyer present during questioning?"

"I need to speak to Brittany first."

Brittany was brought back to the room; Kerri and I waited in the hall.

"Where are Elena and Taylor?"

"In two other interview rooms with their parents. They're waiting for their lawyers to arrive."

"Not cooperating?"

"Too early to know, but let's say I have extra leverage to use with them."

"Which is?"

"They're being charged with the sale and distribution of controlled substances to other minors."

"How'd you pull that off?"

"Got another student to make two separate buys this week while wearing a wire and being videotaped."

"Really? How did you—Wait a minute. Didn't you say your daughters went to Sacred Heart? Did you—?"

Kerri actually blushed. "Yes. I used my oldest as a CI. Hopefully, that will never come out. I showed both the Carreras and the Gatwicks video of the sales. Told them I had an ADA ready to deal on the drug charges for the girls' complete cooperation on the sex and pornography issue."

"Wow. You're tough."

"My primary goal is to stop children from being exploited and sexually abused. I do what I need to do."

"You brought in two other minors. Were they with these girls?"

"No, they're two 15-year-old boys from a public school. Somehow my surveillance team missed seeing them, or we'd have had to move up the raid. It appears they were involved in a similar scheme as Elena and Taylor."

"What about the three women you arrested. How were they involved?"

"The women may be collateral damage. Won't be sure until after everyone's interviewed and we've gone through the evidence. They're Cramer College students, all over 18. They were making adult porn videos in another part of the house when we went in. Unless I can connect them to the child porn, they'll be released."

The door opened. It was obvious that both mother and daughter had been crying. The laptop on the table was open.

"Brittany will answer any question you have."

"Are you sure that you wouldn't like to have a lawyer present during questioning?"

"That won't be necessary. Thank you." Melanie's voice had taken on a resolve she hadn't shown previously.

"Would you like me to stay?"

"Thank you, Rachel, but no. Brittany and I will handle it from here. This is our mess to clean up. Thank you for coming with me. I truly appreciate it."

Before leaving the police station, I got a panic call from Lauren.

"Ms. Cord? This is Lauren Kennedy. I think we're in big trouble. It's nearly 4:30 and Elena, Taylor and Brittany haven't come back to the mall yet. I can't reach them by phone either. I don't know what's happening, but my dad's going to be here at 5:00. I've no idea what to tell him."

"Lauren, calm down. Elena, Taylor and Brittany were picked up this morning when the police raided the house the girls were at."

"Oh, my God! They were arrested?"

"Not yet, but they are in police custody and are being questioned. Their parents are here too."

"Oh, my God."

"I only know this because Mrs. Upchurch asked me to come with her to the station to pick up Brittany. I don't know what's being said in the interview rooms with detectives, but I think the whole story will come out sometime tonight."

"Oh, my God. We are in big trouble."

"Quite probably. I would be surprised if your parents and Emily's parents aren't called later."

"What should we do?"

"I suggest you meet your dad and have him take you, Emily and Maria to your house as there is no one at the Carreras'. Then I suggest you three tell your parents everything you know. And I mean everything. This is no time to hold anything back."

"Oh, God."

"I'm sorry, Lauren. Elena and Taylor were treading in dangerous waters. This was bound to happen sooner than later."

When **I got home,** I gave Wendy a long hug and gave her an update.

"Doesn't look like you had a good day. Thought you'd be pleased with the way things went."

"I am and I'm not. I'm pleased with the arrests, and the media coverage, and my contributions to making it happen. But there are some disillusioned families tonight facing hard realities; that makes me sad. What's even sadder is that those videos and photographs of Elena and Taylor and Brittany are still being seen by who knows how many perverts."

"I thought you said that website was being taken down."

"It is. But did they post them elsewhere too? How many people downloaded those videos and pictures? How many reposted them to other websites? How long will it take to close those sites down? It's like an epidemic without a complete cure. Once on the Web, always on the Web."

There didn't seem to be anything else to say. Silence lingered.

"Would you like some wine?"

"Right now I feel like something stronger, but wine would be nice. So, what are we ordering for dinner?"

"I thought Indian, if that's all right. Mildly spiced for you, of course."

"Sounds great. How about another hug, though; then let's start that bottle of wine."

Twenty-Five

Tanya's **Evening and Late** Nite Reports included interviews with Tiger Lil from the Lillith Society on child exploitation. Tanya also promised a three-part feature starting Monday night on child Internet porn, the commercial sex industry, and domestic human trafficking. As promised, she made no reference to me or to any official or unofficial source of the original tip.

Andy's Sunday feature was even more detailed with lots of stats that Andy has a way of explaining and putting into easily understandable context. It was saddening to see just how prevalent the problem was nationally. His feature included interviews with Tiger Lil, Kerri Trujillo, and Officer Denise Brody from Missing Persons, as well as with local child specialists.

Sunday and Monday pretty much passed without incident. Unfortunately, there were no verifiable updates or sightings of Paul Beauxdreaux.

Late Tuesday afternoon Frank called to say he'd gotten separate reports that Beauxdreaux's truck may have been spotted in eastern Illinois and in southern Indiana. There were no positive sightings of Beauxdreaux however.

"You think he's given up and headed home?"

"Hard to say, Rachel. Looks that way, and he is due back from his hunting trip."

"But . . ."

"Right, but. Looks are deceiving. The way this guy came after you again after being injured, and the personal vendetta he seems to be on, I can't picture him giving up now. So until we know for sure that he's been picked up —"

"I shouldn't take any chances."

"I certainly wouldn't at this point."

I called Wendy at her bank with the latest news. Beaudreaux's truck being sighted out of state gave her some relief, but she understood it was too soon to let down our guard. Still, she thought we should go out for dinner and maybe catch Sonny's act at the Basement Bistro afterwards. We decided on Nicoletti's Italian as it was close to both us and to the Bistro.

We enjoyed our meal and left the restaurant in good cheer. Wendy spotted a homeless guy at the corner in a grimy cammie jacket with a sign: "Spare a Buck for a Vet." She walked over and gave him $20. We then headed for my car in the parking lot.

There was no warning. I heard the shot at the same time I felt it punching me in the back throwing me against Wendy. I shoved her aside, began turning and drawing my gun to return fire. I glimpsed what looked like blood spattering from Wendy's head and heard a second shot. I saw the shooter, the homeless guy, holding a gun in his left hand and bracing it with his bandaged right hand as he came toward us. I raised my gun, but his third shot hit me in my upper arm and my gun fell to the pavement. The fourth shot hit me squarely in the chest. Heard an echo or a fifth shot. Not sure.

I lay on my back choking; hard to breathe; pain just beginning to register; eyes blurring; darkening indigo sky with a few pinkish purplish cirrus clouds capturing the last of sunset overhead; my hand spasmodic, fumbling for my gun

170

somewhere nearby. Where was Wendy? Was she alive? Had to move. Couldn't.

A shadowy figure looming, cutting off the sky, leaning close; spit on my face.

"It's over, bitch! Alan sends his regards. Says he'll meet you in Hell."

A gun muzzle.

Bang!

Bang!

Bang!

Bang!

Bang!

Sky again and silence. Then another shadow. Wendy leaning close, her face dripping tears and blood onto mine.

"Help's coming."

Epilogue

"**There are strange things** done in the midnight sun by the men who moil for gold; the Arctic trails have their secret tales that would make your blood run—"

"Not my favorite poet," I dryly complained interrupting Wendy's recitation.

"Not erotically arousing enough, I suppose." Wendy, her head half-bandaged and holding a slim book, smiled from her chair across the room.

"Just not ready for cremation tales. And please don't switch to hearing buzzing flies, either, even if I am fonder of Emily."

Wendy stiffly rose from her chair, came to the bed, and gave me a glass of water to sip. Then she leaned down and kissed me. *That* was more erotically arousing. Her robe parted and I saw the dark bruise where one of Beauxdreaux's shots had hit the protective vest she had worn. I winced in sympathy and also at the pain from my own protective vest bruisings and from the shot to my arm.

I reached up and tenderly touched the bandage on the side of her head. Beauxdreaux's shot had grazed her. Lots of blood, a ruined hairdo, but no lasting damage. We kissed again as Wendy slipped out of her robe, pulled back the covers, and slid into bed beside me. She cuddled close, a hand sliding between my thighs.

173

"Should we be doing this, this soon?"

"Cuddling? Why not? The hospital released us, didn't they? I can't see any reason not to as long as we're careful and don't over do it, do you?"

"Definitely not." I ignored the sharp twinges as I turned to better place my arms around her. "Besides, I haven't thanked you enough for saving our lives."

Wendy closed her eyes.

"Still upset you had to shoot him?"

She sighed. "More a guilt that I was pleased after I did it."

"I know. Perfectly normal reaction."

"So they tell me." Her hand came up and lightly traced the contours of my face. "Do you still feel it—guilt, I mean—about the people you've had to kill?"

"Some days more than others. Mostly, I've learned to live with it. Mostly."

I moved my hand to stroke between her legs; felt the warmth and wetness as she responded to my touch.

"But now's not the time to think of that."

No, now was the time to be thankful we were both alive. I kissed her softly on her lips, her chin, her neck and carefully began—*ouch*—to slither down beneath the covers.

As **Wendy and I recovered** until time to head for Florida for my surgery, I gave more thought to Andy's suggestion we write a book. I decided I had healed enough to face what happened in my life. I invited him over and, for the first time, I told Andy the full story of that night at Tierney's and the fallout afterward.

"Wow. That's going to be hard to write."

"I know. That's why I've avoided telling it. But I'm not sure there's any way to avoid it or leave it out. It happened, and it's an indelible part of my life."

"Well, let's worry about that when we get that far. How about we start with your search for Linda Miller?"

That first meeting lasted four hours with Andy recording what I said and him taking notes. We met several more times. At our last meeting before leaving for Florida, Andy showed me an outline of how he thought the book should go and said he'd work on a first draft while I was away. I told him I didn't much care for the title *Confessions of Madame Gumshoe*.

"Makes me sound like a brothel owner in sneakers rather than a PI."

We tossed ideas back and forth when Andy picked up one of my cards.

"How about *Life's a Bitch. So Am I.?*"

"By Rachel Cord as told to Andy Walther, of course."

"Who else?"

Elena, Taylor and Brittany were not prosecuted for prostitution but were treated like the victims they truly were. Elena and Taylor did plead guilty, however, in Juvenile Court to one count of the sale and distribution of a controlled substance or fake substance. Turned out that much of what they were selling contained no marijuana at all. Their two-year sentences were suspended and commuted to probation pending their full cooperation in the cases of the adults involved, and successful completion of community service and educational treatment programs. Successful completion of probation would also expunge their convictions.

Brittany, Emily, Lauren and Maria were not charged with any crimes, but their parents and guardians imposed similar punishments of community service and enrollment into educational programs for their complicity.

Brittany is no longer a *Heather* wannabe. She and her mother have joined the Lillith Society where Brittany speaks to others of the dangers young girls can get entrapped into.

Melanie Upchurch is becoming an expert in researching Internet child pornography. She has already been responsible for eight websites being taken down.

All of the adults charged in the raid near Cramer College made deals and pled guilty. Sentences ranged from probation to five years in prison. All will need to register as sex offenders. Information they provided led to 23 further arrests; more are pending additional evidence.

Paul Harvey Beauxdreaux's body was claimed by his family and returned to his home for burial. Alan Wilson remains on Death Row.

Wendy, Clare, my friend and former Army commander Helen Abernathy, and I laughingly left The All-Star Revue in Orlando, Florida. It was a perfect birthday evening of song, dance and comedy before my long-awaited surgery. We rounded the corner toward the parking lot.

From an alley that separated The All-Star Revue from another club, we heard quarreling and glanced over.

"Oof!"

"Not laughing now, funnyman, are you?"

Two men were beating a third against a wall. Helen rushed forward pulling something from her purse. I followed rolling the program I carried into a tight cylinder.

"Hey!" Helen screamed. "Back away."

"Get lost, bitch."

Helen held up her ID and shield. "Police. I said, back away."

The guy turned and swung at Helen. The other guy tried running past me. I jammed the rolled-up program hard into his gut, stopping him, but the shock to my still recovering arm made me gasp. I tripped him and pinned him to the ground by sitting on him.

Helen, looking very much like the kick-ass MP captain and "African Queen" as we secretly called her back in the day, stood calmly with a foot firmly planted on the neck of the guy who had attacked her.

"Fuck," he moaned. "You broke my arm."

"That's not all I'll break if you ruined this dress. Now shut up and lie still."

Helen opened her cell phone. "This is Detective Helen Abernathy, Gainesville Florida Police Department. There's been an assault in the alley between The All-Star Revue and the Haw Haw Club here in Orlando. I'm not sure of the address. We have two suspects in custody. We need units and medical assistance."

As Helen filled in the police dispatcher, I looked over to where Wendy and Clare dabbed blood from the face of the victim. Just my luck: Jacky Fry. Looked like all he got was a busted nose and a shiner. Too bad. I still think Fry should be jailed for impersonating a comic—not these two clowns for doing a public service. Still, better them than me. I've waited too long. Three more days and it's bye-bye, albatross.

Author's note

The sexual exploitation and trafficking of young girls and women is an on-going problem in this country and around the world; as well is the never-ending need to change established attitudes toward these women who should be treated as victims and not as the willing participants they are perceived to be. Organizations like GEMS in New York City—upon which my fictional Lillith Society is based—are doing what they can to change laws and attitudes and to help these victims. To learn more, I highly recommend the memoir, *Girls Like Us*, by Rachel Lloyd who founded GEMS and is a former victim herself.

Rape and sexual abuse are horrid, haunting, ugly events that should never be tolerated. If you are—or someone you know is—a victim of rape, abuse or incest, call **1-800-656-HOPE** or access the **National Sexual Assault Online Hotline (https://hotline.rainn.org/online/terms-of-service.jsp)** direct. Available also in Spanish.

RAINN (Rape, Abuse & Incest National Network) has helped more than 1.8 million sexual assault survivors toward recovery and has increased the number of victims reporting attacks to the police. Some called minutes after being attacked; others called decades later. RAINN was there to help each one because of active supporters. Learn more at www.rainn.org.

A Bonus Rachel Cord Excerpt follows

RACHEL CORD
Confidential Investigations

Queen of Tarts

R. E. Conary

Coming This Fall

Monday, March 22, 2010

One

I **glanced out my** office windows. Not a lot was happening. There'd been a bit of rain overnight and it was still overcast and chilly. I had no appointments and the two open cases resting on school desks were waiting for information before I could close them out. I went back to reading an article in *PI Magazine* on interviewing people with personality disorders when Doris Garrity brought in my mail.

"There are two checks you need to endorse for deposit, Rachel. The rest is basically junk mail."

"Thanks, Doris. Just put them on the desk."

"Rachel? Are you busy?"

"Not really. What do you need?"

Doris came and sat in the other loveseat. "A neighbor of mine, Mr. Carlson, is in the hospital. He's in critical condition and in a coma."

"Sorry to hear that. What happened to him?"

"Someone broke into his home Thursday night, attacked him and ransacked the house. He wasn't found until the next morning when Edna Duquesne, who lives next door, saw his front door open but didn't see him in the yard. That's very unusual. She found him on his living room floor and called 911. The police think it was a burglary gone bad."

"And you're not sure?"

"I don't know. There haven't been any burglaries in our

neighborhood in quite some time that I know of. He's an old man. Lives alone. Doesn't associate with anyone except Edna. I doubt he has anything worth stealing. Nothing gets delivered there. He walks everywhere. Doesn't own a car. Why pick on him?"

"Good question. Have the police provided any information."

"Not really. According to Edna, the police have little to go on, as they haven't been able to speak with him. With the house a mess, she says, it's hard to tell what's missing."

"Are you asking me to look into it?"

"Would you?"

"What do you think I can do that the police aren't doing?"

"I don't know. It's just so frightening. The thought that someone is breaking into houses in our neighborhood and hurting people is scary. Everyone's on edge."

"I would think so. Have you spoken with the police?"

"Yes. An Officer Drake stopped by Friday evening. He was going door-to-door asking everyone about anything suspicious the night before. We hadn't heard anything. He didn't have much to tell us. He gave us a card and said to call the detective in charge if we thought of anything. But there's been no news, and it's Monday already."

"Who's the detective?"

"Detective Paul Wodehouse. Here's his card."

"I've met him. He works out of West Division. I can call him, if you'd like, but doubt I'll get anything you don't have already, if that much. My butting in isn't usually welcome."

"Anything you find out would be appreciated."

"Do you know Carlson's full name?"

"Edna calls him Ray. Might be short for Raymond."

"Okay. I'll let you know what I find."

"Thanks."

Doris left and I stared at the card she'd given me. *Paul G. Woodhouse.* I'd met him twice, no, three times. The first was at Lt. Ed Montero's promotion party a few years back. Dean

Lockhart introduced us. The other times were in the past year when I had information to pass along. Maybe he'd reciprocate now. I recognized one of the two numbers on the card as the police department's main line. I called the other one.

"Detective Wodehouse. May I help you?"

"Good morning, Detective. This is Rachel Cord. We haven't spoken in several months. How are you?"

"Aside from being overworked and underpaid, I'm alive. How 'bout you?"

"Doing well, actually."

"Glad to hear it. You have something you want to share with me?"

"Not at the moment. I'm hoping there's some information you could give me."

"And what would that be?"

"Ray Carlson was attacked in his home last week, and I understand you're the lead detective. Have there been any developments?"

"What's your interest? Do you know the vic?"

"I've never met him. A woman who does secretarial work for me is a neighbor. Her family's worried they could be attacked too. Can you tell me anything?"

"Not a lot. He's still unconscious, but has been upgraded to stable. So I haven't been able to talk to him. I'll be checking on him again later today. Right now, we think the intent was robbery. That morning he withdrew cash from an ATM at a nearby grocery store. Someone may have seen him and followed him home. That may be the reason. It's hard to say for sure. We didn't find any cash at his home, and his wallet is missing."

"Why do you say it's 'hard to say' if that's the reason or not?"

"Because his ATM receipt said he only took out $40, and he spent nearly half that at the grocery store. That's not a big haul for such a violent break-in."

"True. But would the robber know that's all he took out?

Maybe he was standing where he could see the ATM screen and thought it was $400, not $40."

"I suppose that's a possibility. Carlson's place was tossed as if the perp thought there was more cash somewhere. Or something else worth taking."

"Like what?"

"No idea. Most of the stuff in the house was outdated and still there. And the mess makes it hard to tell what could be missing. Just keeping options open. The perp worked the old man senseless then trashed the place. That's all I know for sure."

"Do you think this was a specific attack, and others in the neighborhood aren't in danger?"

"That's what my gut says. This wasn't a break-in. Carlson must have opened the door. Why, I don't know yet. Maybe he knew his attacker. Still, I can't rule out the possibility of more robberies. Depends on what the perp was really after and whether he got it or not. Patrols have been increased in the area, just in case."

"I see your problem. Anything you can tell me about the victim?"

"Name is Raymond Henry Carlson, white male; turned 76 in February; Army retired. Inherited the house when his mother died in '87. Haven't discovered any next-of-kin yet. Seems to be a loner. His next-door neighbor, Mrs. Edna Duquesne, is his emergency contact."

"Is the house still a crime scene?"

"Why? You want to go snooping to see what we missed?"

"Who, me? Not at all. Just thought Mrs. Duquesne and some of the other neighbors might want to clean the place for his return."

"Very considerate of you. Now's not good. I may want to go back myself for another look. I'll let Mrs. Duquesne know when she can tidy up. Anything else?"

"No, thank you. I'll let you get back to work."

"Appreciate it. Oh, if you do come across anything I

should know, call me."

"Definitely."

There wasn't much new information, but I gave Doris the rundown, anyway.

"I'm glad to hear his condition is better. He's always been a good neighbor. Never any problems in the nearly nine years we've lived there. So you don't think there's any danger?"

"Wodehouse thinks it's a one-off. But who knows for sure."

"Any chance you can investigate it further? I can pay you."

Doris took out her checkbook.

"Put that away."

"Rachel—"

"Look. My current cases are caught up except for the two I'm waiting for info on. I don't have any scheduled appointments. So I can spend a few hours checking some things. I can't really interfere with a police investigation, but I'll try to find out what I can. There may well be no need for you to pay me."

"Okay."

"What can you tell me about Carlson?"

"Not a whole lot. Edna's the best one to talk to. Except for Carlson, she's lived on the block the longest. She knew his mother. We live three doors down on the opposite side. I'd see him often working in his rose garden or cutting his grass with an old rotary push mower. Always polite, but quiet. Keeps to himself. Must be in his late seventies, but spry and in good health for his age. Strong too. Couple of years ago, Tina, my youngest, fell off her bike by his house and hurt her leg. He carried her home. Wasn't even bothered he got blood on his clothes."

I glanced at the family photo Doris kept on her desk. Her two boys had dark chocolate skin like she did but were tall like their father. The two girls were much lighter. Her husband, Bud, was white with a radiant smile."

"What can you tell me about the neighborhood?"

"Mostly quiet. I would have said 'safe' except for what happened to Mr. Carlson. Capri Estates is a sought-after area. Property values are sky high. So are our taxes. But I wouldn't live anywhere else now. We bought before everyone else found it. Back in 2001. Moved in on nine-eleven. Can you believe that? Not a clue about what happened till late in the afternoon. I got a new house, and 3,000 people died."

"Somehow, I don't think the two events are related."

"No, but it sure put a damper on our excitement for awhile. Anyway, Capri was a late-forties project aimed at returning veterans. The original houses were two bedrooms, living room and eat-in kitchens, with attached one-car garages and small front and back yards. Pastel colors and red tiled roofs. More than half the houses now have converted garages as extra bedrooms or family rooms. Some, like ours, were completely renovated with a second story added. Others, like my friend Anita's, added on the back. Trees planted in the fifties tower over the entire area and line the streets. Carlson's house is still original, I believe. I've never been in it."

"Do you have Mrs. Duquesne's number? Do you think she's available to talk with me?"

"Edna's a retired teacher. Like Carlson, she lives alone. Her husband died some years ago, and her kids are grown and on their own. Here's her home number and address. If she's not home, she may be at the hospital with Carlson."

I called Mrs. Duquesne's number and got an answering machine. I didn't leave a message. Taking the chance she was at the hospital, I drove there. There was a flower and gift shop in the lobby where I picked up a small bouquet of assorted roses, carnations and mums in a mug to cheer Carlson when he awoke. After getting directions, I went to his room on the 6th floor. An elderly, black woman sat in a visitor's chair reading. Carlson appeared to be sleeping. His face was heavily bruised. He was hooked up to various machines and had an oxygen tube clipped to his nose.

"Hi, are you Mrs. Duquesne? I'm Rachel Cord. Doris Garrity sends her sympathies to Mr. Carlson."

I showed her the flowers. She rose from her chair and set the book aside.

"That's very kind of Doris, and you for bringing them. They're lovely. I'm certain Ray will enjoy them."

She took the flowers and placed them next to a bouquet of light pink roses on a table by the window where they could be seen but out of the way. I looked at Carlson. His face was puffy and so heavily bruised he looked more black than white. Though the bruising was beginning to turn a sickly yellow at the edges. His forearms were equally bruised as if he had tried to defend himself and bruises on his wrists looked like he'd been tied. I turned to Mrs. Duquesne.

"How is he?"

"Better. He opened his eyes for the first time about an hour ago and smiled at me. His doctor checked him. He has a concussion among his other injuries. Needs rest mostly. I was reading to him when he awoke. He's sleeping now. Rachel Cord? You're the private detective Doris speaks about, aren't you?"

"Yes, I am. Doris asked me to help find out why Carlson was attacked. May I ask you some questions?"

"I don't know that I know anything that would help."

"I understand you've known him a long time. Just telling me about him could be helpful."

"He's resting. I'd hate for our talking to disturb him."

"We could talk in the visitors lounge or go to the cafeteria. Have you had lunch? I'd be happy to buy."

"Thank you, but I brought sandwiches. We could have coffee, though. I know the nurses will keep an eye on him."

We sat at the windows in the cafeteria looking out on a courtyard. Mrs. Duquesne with her tuna salad sandwiches and coffee and me with a burger, fries and diet soda.

"Exactly how long have you known Raymond Carlson,

Mrs. Duquesne?"

"Please, call me Edna. I stopped being Mrs. Duquesne when I retired. Horus and I bought our home in 1984. That's when we met Ray and his mother, Abigail. She had Alzheimer's. Ray took care of her."

"Had he always lived with his mother?"

"Oh, no. He retired from the Army, in 1980, I think. I remember he mentioned Arizona. He moved home a couple years later when Abigail needed help. She was a sweet lady. On good days her mind was still sharp. She taught English at Horace Mann High School in the fifties, sixties and early seventies. I taught English and literature there for three years until they closed it in '86. Then I moved to John F. Kennedy High School until I retired. Abigail and I shared many memories of Horace Mann. She loved it so. It's now a business plaza, you know."

"Yes, I know. That's where I have my office."

"Really? How nice. Which room is yours? Maybe it was mine."

"Room 222. Actually only half of the room. The developers split many of the larger classrooms into two offices."

"That was Pete Haynes' old room. He taught history."

"I love the large windows." I sipped my soda. "How long did Carlson care for his mother?"

"Let me see. She died in 1989. It was Mother's Day. I remember that. She'd been in hospice about six weeks. I was there with Ray when she passed. I guess about seven years."

"Must have been hard for him."

"It was. Hardly left the house for more than a year after. Let the yard go to pot. Then one day, all of a sudden, he was out in the yard mowing, trimming, pruning and all. Came over and asked me if there were anything of his mother's I'd like to have. Said Salvation Army was coming to take everything else. She had a pair of vases she knew I liked. I took those and a large photograph of Horace Mann High. I still have them. He gave everything else away, even the furniture. Bought new stuff for himself. Painted the house inside and out."

"And he's stayed there ever since?"

"Pretty much. Went away a few times to Arizona in the nineties for a couple of months at a time. We watered his plants and mowed the lawn for him then. Since 2000 he hasn't gone anywhere. We've kind of looked out for each other after my Horus died."

Edna filled me in on the family history as told to her by Abigail on her good days and brought me up to speed on Carlson's day-to-day activities.

Carlson's house was among the first in the development built in 1948 during the post-war boom. his parents, Henry and Abigail, bought the house new after moving from Ohio. His father was a World War II veteran, who completed his engineering degree on the GI Bill, and moved the family here to join the local aeronautical industry. Raymond was 14 at the time.

Over the decades the neighborhood went through many changes from exclusively white to predominantly black to mostly Hispanic by the late nineties. Local businesses changed hands and many closed giving the area a rundown feel. Then in 2003, it's tree-lined streets piqued new interest and affordable prices created a resurgence. The Carlson home was one of very few still owned by the original family.

Raymond Carlson was a creature of habit. He kept primarily to himself. When he was working in the yard or out on one of his daily walks, he would nod and smile, or wave, to people he saw; might even offer a "Good morning" or a rarer "Hi, how you doing?" But that was about it. He rarely stopped to chat. If he did, it would be about everyday things. Never about himself. Most people called him "Old Man Carlson," though not to his face.

Besides his daily walk around the neighborhood, he would walk to Amigos twice a week for lunch. The staff there knew him as *Señor* Ray. He spoke passable Spanish. Once a week, he walked to the library, and twice a month walked the twelve blocks to Piggly Wiggly with his handcart. There he'd use the ATM machine, have lunch next door at Paula's Café or at the Kabob House across the parking lot, do his grocery shopping and then walk home.

Edna had no idea why someone wanted to hurt or rob him. We went back upstairs. A nurse was coming out of Carlson's room and spoke to Edna.

"He's awake but will probably nod off again. Doctor Adams will check in around four."

"Thank you."

Carlson's eyes opened when we entered the room. He tried to smile slightly to Edna and his hand raised a few inches from the bed. Edna took his hand in hers.

"You're going to be okay. Ray, this is Rachel Cord. She's a friend of Doris Garrity, the woman just down the street." He nodded. "She's going to help find who did this to you."

Carlson's eyes shifted to me.

"I'm sorry to bother you, Mr. Carlson. I know you need to rest, but do you know who did this to you?"

He shook his head 'no.'

"Do you know what he wanted?"

He raised his hand to show two fingers.

"Are you saying there were two of them?"

He nodded.

"Both men?"

He shook his head and held up one finger.

"One man? The other was a woman?"

He nodded.

"Were they black or white?"

He held up two fingers.

"White?"

He nodded then held up one finger.

"One was white but the other one wasn't black?"

He nodded.

"Hispanic or Asian, maybe?"

He nodded and held up one finger.

"Hispanic. Was the man or woman Hispanic?"

He raised two fingers.

"Okay. The man was white and the woman Hispanic, is that right?"

He nodded.

"And you didn't know them, right?"

He nodded.

"Do you know what they wanted?"

He nodded.

"Was it cash?"

Carlson shook his head then licked his lips and tried to speak. Nothing came out but a couple grunts. He looked over to the counter and tried to point. Edna went to the counter and poured some water in a glass and held it for him to sip through a straw. He nodded to her and smiled. He looked at me.

"G-g-go-o," was all he managed. He began breathing heavily and closed his eyes for a moment.

"That's all right, Mr. Carlson. Don't strain yourself. Can you still nod?"

He nodded.

"Okay. Did they get what they wanted?"

He shook his head and shrugged slightly.

"Is that 'no' or 'you don't know'?"

His eyes drooped and he closed them for several moments before opening them again. He held up two fingers.

"Then you don't know, correct?"

He nodded. His breathing was still labored and he closed his eyes again. In a few moments it was obvious he had fallen asleep.

"Edna, do you have any idea what he was trying to say?"

"I'm not sure. It sounded like 'go' and something with an 'O'."

"That's what I heard too. But 'go-O' what? Go out somewhere? Go over somewhere? Go on something? Maybe he was trying to say a single word. He was stuttering trying to get it out. Maybe something like 'goal' or 'goat'. Doesn't look like he can tell us right now. Did you notice anything in particular missing from his house?"

"No, I never thought to look with Ray lying there like that. Everything was a mess. And after the ambulance took him away, the police closed the house up. I haven't been able to go back in."

I looked back at Carlson. His breathing seemed normal to me and he was sleeping soundly. It was frustrating that he couldn't communicate better. What did the thieves want if not cash? I really wanted a look in his house.

"Edna, would you . . . never mind. Excuse me a moment, please."

I went out in the hall and called Wodehouse.

"This is Rachel. If you haven't been told yet, Raymond Carlson has regained consciousness. He's weak and can't communicate well."

"I was just leaving to go see him."

"He's sleeping again. No idea when he'll reawaken. I did find out that he was attacked by two people: a white male and an Hispanic female. And I don't think they were looking for cash."

"What makes you say that?"

"He could only communicate by nodding or shaking his head. When I asked if it were cash, he indicated no. He wasn't able to tell me what it was or if they found it. I think my questions wore him out."

"Great. A white male with a Hispanic female isn't much help in this town."

"True. Sorry. Look, I'd like to take Mrs. Duquesne back to Carlson's house and see if she can see what's missing. And if nothing is, it's possible his attackers may return."

"That's a good point. We've had patrols checking the house regularly but not under constant surveilance. I'm glad you're asking permission and not sneaking over there."

"You said not to and that you planned to look again. I'm hoping you'll let me tag along."

"Okay. Let's meet there in half-an-hour. Don't go in without me."

"Wouldn't think of it."

www.ingramcontent.com/pod-product-compliance
Lightning Source LLC
Chambersburg PA
CBHW071511170626
46811CB00007B/2811